Saving Kabul Corner

Also by N. H. Senzai

Shooting Kabul

Saving Kabul Corner

N. H. Senzai

A Paula Wiseman Book

Simon & Schuster Books for Young Readers

NEW YORK LONDON TORONTO SYDNEY NEW DELHI

An imprint of Simon & Schuster Children's Publishing Division
1230 Avenue of the Americas, New York, New York 10020

This book is a work of fiction. Any references to historical events, real people, or real places are used fictitiously. Other names, characters, places, and events are products of the author's imagination, and any resemblance to actual events or places or persons, living or dead, is entirely coincidental.

SIMON & SCHUSTER BOOKS FOR YOUNG READERS
is a trademark of Simon & Schuster, Inc.
For information about special discounts for bulk purchases, please contact Simon & Schuster Special Sales at 1-866-506-1949 or business@simonandschuster.com.
The Simon & Schuster Speakers Bureau can bring authors to your live event. For more information or to book an event, contact the Simon & Schuster Speakers Bureau at 1-866-248-3049 or visit our website at www.simonspeakers.com.
Also available in a Simon & Schuster Books for Young Readers hardcover edition
Book design by Chloë Foglia
The text for this book is set in Bembo.
Manufactured in the United States of America
0216 OFF
First Simon & Schuster Books for Young Readers paperback edition February 2015
2 4 6 8 10 9 7 5 3
The Library of Congress has cataloged the hardcover edition as follows:
Senzai, N. H.
Saving Kabul Corner / N. H. Senzai.
pages cm
"A Paula Wiseman Book."
Summary: Twelve-year-old Ariana, a tomboy, and her ladylike cousin Laila, recently arrived from Afghanistan, do not get along but they pull together when a rival Afghani grocery store opens, rekindling an old family feud and threatening their family's livelihood.
ISBN 978-1-4424-8494-8 (hardcover)
ISBN 978-1-4424-8496-2 (eBook)
ISBN 978-1-4424-8495-5 (pbk)
1. Afghan Americans—California—San Francisco Bay Area—Juvenile fiction.
[1. Afghan Americans—Fiction. 2. Grocery trade—Fiction. 3. Vendetta—Fiction. 4. Immigrants—Fiction. 5. Family life—California—Fiction. 6. San Francisco Bay Area (Calif.)—Fiction. 7. Mystery and detective stories.] I. Title. PZ7.S47953Sav 2014
[Fic]—dc23
2013005211

In memory of Ammi.

Every day, you are missed.

Acknowledgments

THE HAPPY NEWS THAT *Saving Kabul Corner* had been accepted for publication was tempered soon after by the sorrow of my mother's death. After a brave battle with cancer, she finally succumbed on September 9, 2012. Ammi, as we called her, was my greatest supporter, and her gentle encouragement buoyed me to write. As family and friends came together to mourn her loss, my agent, Michael Bourret; publisher, Paula Wiseman; and editor, Alexandra Penfold, not only offered their condolences but also let me know that I could take as long as I wanted to write the book. But in the end I kept to my tight deadline and completed the novel. It proved to be an anchor that kept me rooted during that difficult and trying time—so I thank all three for their compassion and support. A critical ally in helping me bring the manuscript to life was Hena Khan, author extraordinaire and invaluable critique partner. Continued thanks to my family, in particular to Farid and Zakaria for putting up with me during the writing process and enjoying picnic dinners composed of peanut butter, jelly, and crackers. A special thanks to all the readers who, after finishing *Shooting Kabul*, wanted to know what happened to Mariam. I hope that I have answered that question!

CONTENTS

Saving Kabul Corner

1

Perfectly Awful

ARIANA HAPHAZARDLY SHOVELED PISTACHIOS into a bin and tried not to glare at her cousin, Laila, who knelt near the cash register, carefully stacking jars of cherry jam. Laila's long-lashed aquamarine eyes glowed with concentration, and a thoughtful frown marred her face, which was framed with silky brown hair roped together in a neat braid. After finishing her task quickly and efficiently, Laila floated down the aisle toward a stack of boxes that had just been delivered. She wasn't stampeding like a rhino, which Ariana had often been told she resembled. Ariana could just imagine her mother's voice ringing in her ears.

Ariana jaan, please try to be more ladylike. . . . Walk, don't gallop. . . . Watching Laila glide down the checkered linoleum floor, Ariana fumed. *She really is perfect.*

Nearly thirteen, Laila could cook like a proper Afghan girl, as well as sew, embroider, recite classical poetry, and sing in three languages—Pukhto, Farsi, and English. She'd also been the top student at her all-girls school back in Kabul. Only a few months younger, Ariana could barely toast a Pop-Tart without burning it, or sew a button on a shirt without pricking her finger on the needle. As Ariana surreptitiously watched Laila, she tried to squash the hot, throbbing sensation blossoming near her heart. She couldn't help it. *I hate her guts. Which are probably also perfect.*

With a dejected sigh Ariana glowered at the pistachios that had escaped the bin, a hint of guilt blossoming in her heart. Laila was her cousin, and it wasn't Laila's fault that she was, well, *perfect.* But ever since Laila had arrived and moved into their tiny town house with them on Peralta Boulevard a month ago, things had changed drastically for Ariana. While Laila's mother had taken Ariana's eldest brother, Zayd's, bedroom, Laila had moved into Ariana's postage-stamp-size space that she'd already been sharing with their grandmother Hava Bibi. Laila's father was Hava

Bibi's nephew and part of the huge Shinwari clan from which they got their last name. Since Hava Bibi was an elder within a close-knit Afghan family, she was considered to be Laila's grandmother too. The moment Laila and her mother had touched down in San Francisco, their extended family had flown into a frenzy of activity. Every other day there had been a party, welcoming them to their new life in the United States, away from war-torn Afghanistan. Ariana felt like an extra shoe, lying around, trying to find the right foot to fit.

With a muffled sigh Ariana looked away, trying to think of something, anything, to squelch the flood of negative thoughts. Then it flashed before her, the date she'd circled in red on her Peanuts calendar back home—January 27, one hundred and forty-seven days away. That day represented something that she'd hungered for for as long as she could remember—*privacy*. During spring break her parents had taken her and her three brothers down to a new subdivision at the foot of Mission Hills. After touring the model homes, her father, Jamil, had put a down payment on a two-story white stucco house with a red tiled roof. It was their dream house, which they'd been saving up for four years, and her dad made sure there was something for everyone: a modern kitchen with modern steel appliances for her mother, and a huge family room with a brand-new wide screen television so Hava Bibi could watch her Afghan soaps. A spacious backyard jutted out behind the house, and best of all, there was a separate bedroom for each of the four kids. Ariana recalled the blueprints, printed on soft turquoise paper, where her father had pointed out her very own bedroom, overlooking the green hills beyond.

"Hey," grumbled Zayd, interrupting Ariana's daydream. At seventeen he'd appointed himself third in command, after their father and their father's younger brother Uncle Shams, co-owners of the family grocery store, Kabul Corner. "Who's going to eat *those*?" he asked, glaring at the stray nuts on the floor. "Do you think money grows on trees or something?"

Thankfully, she didn't have to answer, because their nine-year-old twin brothers, Omar and Hasan, teetered by, lugging a fifty-pound bag of flour between them.

"Man, can you lift higher?" complained Omar. He was younger than Hasan by two minutes.

"Dude, I'm doing the best I can," grumbled Hasan, his skinny arms trembling.

In their haste to reach the bakery at the back of the

store, they crashed into a shelf, sending a line of cans thudding to the floor.

"Watch it, you two!" yelled Zayd, running toward them.

Laila came running around the corner, carrying an unwieldy box, her head barely visible behind it. "I'll help them," she said. Laila set down the box and grabbed one end of the bag. "Come on, I know you have the muscles, but I'm going to help you navigate to the bakery."

"Thanks," chorused the twins, following her lead.

"Ari!" shouted Zayd, using her nickname, his arms full of cans. "Get with it! The store's about to open. Help Laila with that box."

Before Ariana could get up off the floor, Laila returned to move the box of cashews herself. She avoided Ariana's gaze and focused on reaching the nut bins.

"Thanks for being so helpful around the store," said Zayd, smiling at Laila, then shooting Ariana an irritated look.

"It's no problem," said Laila, giving Zayd a tentative smile. "I like helping out."

"You're totally awesome," said Zayd, ruffling her hair and handing her a scoop.

Steamed at the love fest, Ariana fled to the front of the store, leaving Laila to fill the cashew bin with *perfect* precision, not dropping a single nut. Ariana paused a moment to run her hand along a display of embroidered cushions, letting the soft maroon velvet soothe her fingertips. All around the store she could see the hard work her father and uncle had put in. It was their pride and joy. When Kabul Corner had opened its doors nearly a decade before, it had been the first large Afghan grocery store in the city. With a prime location in central Fremont, the hub of the Afghan community, the store had quickly become *the* place to find spices; freshly baked bread; halal meat, slaughtered according to Islamic regulations; and a good gossip session. She sniffed the warm, sweet scent of cinnamon, mixed in with the earthy smell of cumin, and knelt beside the spice rack to organize it, just as her uncle walked through the door.

"*Salaam alaikum*, Uncle Shams," said Ariana.

"*Walaikum a'salaam, jaan*," said Uncle Shams, narrowing his eyes at the stack of spice packets. "Make sure those are hung properly. Last time, you mixed the cayenne pepper in with the cinnamon. Mrs. Balkh accidently bought the wrong thing and complained to me about it for a week."

"Yes, Uncle Shams," muttered Ariana, ducking away.

"*Salaam*," Uncle Shams greeted Jamil.

"*Walaikum a'salaam*," replied Jamil, who was organizing the cash register.

This was the final countdown. Thirty minutes until opening, and there was still a lot of work to do.

"I'm glad you got more flour," said Jamil. "We were running out."

"I picked it up at Costco," said Uncle Shams, angling his rotund body through the gap to slip behind the counter. He was short and round, in contrast to Ariana's father, who was lanky and slim. People sometimes joked that they couldn't possibly be related. "You won't believe who I ran into while standing in line to pay."

"Who?" asked Jamil.

"General Sahib. Remember him?"

"Of course! He's the one who single-handedly took out two Soviet tanks during the war in '79."

"Yes, that's the one. Well, he just returned from Afghanistan."

"And?" asked Jamil, his eyebrow cocked, expecting more.

"Well," Uncle Shams said with a sigh, "the news's not so good."

Jamil paused from unwrapping a roll of quarters, and Ariana could see him frown. "Of course it isn't good, Shams," he said. "The war in Afghanistan has been going on since 2001. That's more than six years now."

Ariana threaded packets of saffron onto the rack, remembering how the Americans, French, and forty other countries now had troops stationed in Afghanistan.

Uncle Shams sighed. "Well, President Karzai continues to be a disappointment. Everyone had hoped that after his election he'd bring law and order, security and a sense of peace, after decades of war."

Jamil shook his head, his voice gruff. "He's corrupt and ineffectual—so what can we expect but bad news?"

Ariana noticed Laila stiffen at the talk of Afghanistan and start to rub the locket she wore on a short chain around her neck. Ariana usually ignored all the talk about Afghanistan, since it all seemed so far away and had nothing to do with her life here. But watching Laila freeze like a startled rabbit made her pay attention. Laila's father was still in Afghanistan, finishing up his assignment as a translator with the American army. The position could be dangerous, since many considered translators to be traitors because they helped Americans, whom Afghans considered to be foreign invaders.

"But the news this morning was particularly bad. Twenty-three Koreans passing through Ghazni were taken hostage by the Taliban," said Shams in hushed tones.

Taliban. That was a word Ariana knew well. The Taliban were a group of students who'd taken over Afghanistan in 1996 after the invading Soviets had left. Initially they'd brought order and peace to the country, ending years of civil war. But then they'd become corrupt warlords themselves.

"It's as if history is repeating itself," said Jamil. "The Taliban are gaining in strength, and there's fear they'll soon have a foothold in the country."

Laila dropped a bottle of rose water, and as she scrambled to pick it up, Ariana watched her father and Uncle Shams exchange a guilty look.

"Ariana *jaan*," called out her father. "Why don't you and Laila go get us some coffee at the new café. Get something for yourselves, too."

They're trying to get rid of us, Ariana thought. Recognizing an order when she heard one, Ariana took a twenty-dollar bill from her father and exited the front door. "Come on," she said, grudgingly inviting Laila.

Outside, Ariana paused to wait for her cousin. She noticed the big FOR SALE sign on the dilapidated auto parts warehouse behind Wong Plaza. It had been there for a year, and she hoped that it would be turned into something nice—maybe a park, since it was such an eyesore. Ariana plodded ahead, her flip-flops slapping against the pavement. Laila followed, her long tunic-like *kameez* billowing in the faint breeze. She'd been in the United States for only a few weeks, and although they'd taken her shopping for American clothes—jeans, T-shirts, and sneakers—she still preferred to wear Afghan clothes at home. When they went outside, she put jeans on under her *kameez*.

"Hey, Ariana, how's it going?" called out Mr. Martinez, the owner of Juan More Tacos, the restaurant next door.

"Hi, Mr. Martinez," Ariana said, waving. "Everything's good."

"Who's that with you?" he asked.

"My cousin from Afghanistan," said Ariana. "She's staying with us."

"Great. Well, you can both come by for some chips and salsa when you want."

"Thanks. We will," replied Ariana.

They continued down Wong Plaza, the strip mall
where their store was located, anchored on the west
end of the plaza. Laila slowed to admire a fuchsia and
lime-green sari hanging at Milan's Indian Emporium
while Ariana trudged past the Beadery Bead Shoppe
and paused at the sale sign at Well-Read Secondhand
Books. Her nose pressed against the cool window, she
watched Mrs. Smith stack jewel-toned *washi*—thick,
handmade Japanese paper—and shimmering square
pieces of foil in the front display. Ariana's fingers
itched to touch the roughly textured *washi*; at 50 percent off, it would be perfect for making origami.

She gave Mrs. Smith a friendly wave and made a
mental note to come back later with her allowance.
As she waited for Laila to catch up, she caught a
glimpse of her reflection in the window. She wrinkled her nose at the streak of flour in her short, curly
hair. Her mother had tried to tame it into a bob, but
sadly, it resembled a squat bowl perched on top of
her head. A soft T-shirt and fleece sweats enveloped
her sturdy frame; the soft fabric was the only type of
material that didn't cause her to itch and leave angry
red marks on her skin. With a deep sigh she spotted
Laila's slender silhouette behind her and pivoted left,
waving at Mrs. Kim and her pug, Kimchi, at Koo

Koo Dry Cleaning. She noticed that Hooper's Diner still had a FOR LEASE sign hanging out front.

At the bus stop they paused at the light, waiting for their turn to cross. Laila, ever curious about her surroundings, examined the schedule and the line of posters hanging on the wall. Half a dozen faces stared down from multicolored flyers, all asking the residents of Fremont for their vote in the upcoming elections. The light turned green and the girls hurried across the street to the brand-new strip of stores and the Daily Grind Café. The rich aroma of coffee washed over them as they entered, and luckily, the line was short, so Ariana ordered for her father and uncle.

"Two lattes, please. And—," said Ariana, turning to Laila. "Do you want something?"

Laila shrugged, looking around the store with wide, curious eyes.

Ariana bristled. Laila never talked to her much—she seemed to talk to everyone else in the family, but mostly ignored her. Ariana would have blown Laila off, but her father had told her to get something for *both* of them. "How about a hot chocolate?"

"Hot chocolate?" repeated Laila, a look of confusion on her face. "Chocolate that is hot?"

"You'll like it. Give me two small hot chocolates, too," she added to the barista.

"Should we get something for the boys?" asked Laila.

Ariana had forgotten about them. "And a couple of chocolate chip cookies, please."

While the barista whipped up their order, Laila wandered off to look at the ceramic teapot display. Ariana stood watching a group of men playing chess near the front door and spotted a familiar stooped figure, partially hidden behind the coffee display: it was Lucinda Wong, their landlord. The elderly woman was deep in conversation with a short, burly man with a mane of reddish hair. His back was toward Ariana, so she couldn't make out his face. The barista handed her a cardboard tray with the drinks and cookies, and when Ariana turned back, Mrs. Wong and the man were gone.

Ariana watched the look of wonder spread across Laila's face as they exited. Her cousin had taken a tentative sip of the rich, smooth hot chocolate, and whipped cream lined her upper lip.

Ariana couldn't help but smile. "It's good, huh?"

Laila nodded, licking her lip clean.

Eyes shielded from the bright glare of the sun,

Ariana noticed a sign hanging from the empty building at the east end of Wong Plaza. *That's odd*, she thought. The building had been empty for more than a year, and she'd heard her father say that Lucinda had been trying to rent it out for months. Curious, Ariana walked over to read the notice.

Coming Soon!
Pamir Market
Purveyor of fine foods, halal meat, breads, and Afghan
groceries

Ariana stood in front of the sign, her hot chocolate forgotten. A competing Afghan grocery store was opening in the same strip mall as Kabul Corner. *Father and Uncle Shams are not going to like this—not at all*, thought Ariana.

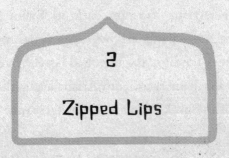

2

Zipped Lips

HIDDEN IN THE HALLWAY, one brown eye peering around the doorway, Ariana spied into the kitchen. Her father sat at the dining table, his cheeks flushed as he listened on the phone. She stood still, straining to listen, but it was hard because of the racket overhead. The twins and Uncle Shams's boys were upstairs, running through the halls, playing Nerf Blasters. Every so often there'd be a loud thump when one of them fell off a bed. *Those dorks better not be in my room*, she thought, seething. When they'd gotten home from the store, Ariana had been tempted to tag along with Zayd to Fadi's house. Fadi's younger sister,

Mariam, was her best friend. They had plans to catch up before school started, but after seeing the worry on her father's face, she'd stayed behind to snoop.

After she'd seen the sign for the new store that morning, Ariana had run back to Kabul Corner, splashing lattes along the way. As soon as she'd told them about the sign, the men had headed over to see the sign for themselves, with Ariana leading the way.

"What the heck?" muttered Uncle Shams, reading the sign.

"This must be some sort of mistake," said Jamil, peering through the window.

"Why would Lucinda do this?" asked Uncle Shams, his cheeks poofing out.

Jamil stepped back. "We need to figure out what's going on before we get all worked up." He turned to Ariana. "Thank you for showing us this, *jaan*, but you need to promise you'll keep quiet about this till your uncle and I know what's going on."

Ariana nodded. She was a little frightened by the sense of apprehension that settled over the men as they walked back to Kabul Corner.

She now watched her father run his hand through his thick, wavy hair as he spoke into the phone; his voice was polite but tense. "But, Lucinda, I don't understand how you could rent the building to another Afghan grocery store. They are in the same business as us."

Jamil listened to Lucinda's response, which went on for a good few minutes. Uncle Shams stood beside him, his eyebrows knitted over stormy eyes, arms clasped over his chest.

"Yes, yes, I know that you need to make the best financial decision, especially during these tough economic times—" He paused with a grimace.

"No, you've been a wonderful landlord—" He stopped, interrupted again.

"Of course you need to do what's best—"

"Yes, well, we are very happy with our location and our lease, but this will be a tremendous challenge for our business—"

"Thank you for your time. . . . Yes, I'll drop by to see you tomorrow. And I hope your son is doing better." With that he hung up the phone.

A loud thump sounded above, and Uncle Shams grabbed the broom and rapped it against the ceiling. "Quiet down, kids!" he yelled, and things stilled, at least momentarily. "What did she say?" he asked.

"She's under great financial pressure, especially after Hooper's Diner closed right after the sewing machine repair shop went under. With no rent coming in, she's strapped for cash."

"This is not good," moaned Uncle Shams, rubbing his temples. "This is *not good*!"

"These Pamir Market people are giving her good rent, which she needs. So it's a business decision, nothing personal."

"Personal, my foot," grumbled Uncle Shams, pacing the kitchen. "All the hard work we've put into Kabul Corner could be ruined!"

Ariana's heart leapt to her throat, and she swallowed hard.

"Now, Shams," said her father. "Don't get worked up. We don't know all the facts."

"Facts?" said Shams, sweat beading along his brow. "What other facts do we need? There is a competing store opening at the opposite end of Wong Plaza, and it could drive us out of business!"

Kabul Corner close? Ariana gasped. She couldn't help it.

Silence descended over the kitchen, and the next few seconds passed with excruciating slowness.

"Ariana, come here," came her father's weary voice.

Darn, she thought, slinking into the kitchen, her head bowed. *I'm going to get it.*

"Eavesdropping is not polite, *jaan*," scolded her father with a look of irritation.

"You're not a little kid anymore," added Uncle Shams, wagging his pudgy finger. "You are a young lady and must behave like one. You don't see Laila hiding, listening to conversations she's not supposed to, do you?"

Ariana's cheeks burned with embarrassment and she shook her head. *Why does perfect Laila have to be dragged into this?*

"Ariana *jaan*, your uncle Shams is right," added her father, making her feel worse. "You're growing up and need to behave properly."

"I'm sorry," said Ariana. "I only wanted to know what was going on. . . . I was worried."

"No need to worry about things that don't concern you," grumbled Uncle Shams.

"Your uncle is right," said her father. "I don't want the rest of the family getting worried unnecessarily. Do you understand?"

Ariana nodded. "Yes, Father."

Dejected, Ariana exited the kitchen, the secret a heavy stone tied across her shoulders. She was tempted to tell someone, anyone, to share the burden, but she knew she couldn't. Her first instinct was to retreat and hide in her room to finish her latest origami project, a miniature zoo. Just thinking about making tiny folds in a soft piece of paper, watching a 3-D figure emerge from a flat page, soothed her nerves. Ever since Ms. Marshall, her second-grade teacher, had taught her class the ancient Japanese art of *ori*, meaning "to fold," and *kami*, "paper," she'd been hooked. She'd already finished the lion, tiger, and bear and needed to work on the elephant next.

As she reached the foot of the stairs, she heard the boys racing through the hall, roughhousing like a troop of baboons.

Omar paused at the top of the steps, his face sweaty. "Hey, Ari," he said, and grinned. "Wanna help us with target practice?"

Ariana gave him a look. *As if.*

"We need someone to stand with an apple on their head," pleaded chubby, freckle-faced Baz, Uncle Shams's eldest son, a year older than the twins.

"No way," she grumbled, and they took off with a disappointed shrug.

Then she remembered that her prized stack of paper wasn't even in her room anymore. She'd had to move it to the garage, since there wasn't enough room for her, Hava Bibi, Laila, and all of their things in the cramped bedroom. Laila's underwear and socks now occupied half the second drawer of the dresser, and the closet was now overflowing with the addition of Laila's *parthuk kameezes* and new American clothes. The corner that had once held Ariana's art supplies was stacked with suitcases. Even her bed was no longer hers. Since Laila was a guest, Ariana slept on the floor, cocooned in a flannel duvet that didn't irritate her skin.

The sound of laughter echoed from the front of the house, breaking into her morose thoughts. *What's so funny?* she thought, wandering over to the living room. Hava Bibi, a white scarf framing her still youthful face, leaned against yellow embroidered cushions, telling a story in rapid-fire Pukhto as the others sat around her. Ariana stood at the door and watched Sara *Khala*, Uncle Shams's wife, laugh so hard that tears streamed down her round cheeks.

"Can you believe it?" asked Hava Bibi, a twinkle in her eye. "The man was so embarrassed by what he'd done, he was never seen in the village again. His *ghayrat* was gone."

Ariana frowned. *Whose ghayrat was gone?* Even though she understood most of what they were saying, she couldn't speak Pukhto very well, and the elders often joked that her accent was terrible. Sometimes, when she didn't understand a word or phrase, they had to translate it for her. Still, she knew that "*ghayrat*" meant "sense of dignity," so whatever had happened must have been pretty bad.

"Where did he go?" asked Laila with barely suppressed excitement. Perched near Hava Bibi's feet, she passed her grandmother some sugared almonds to go with her green tea.

"Some say he went to Kabul and opened a carpet store on Chicken Street."

"Oh, I think I know that store," said Laila, her eyes bright. "Remember, Mother? Our tailor was there, and we used to get *lablabu* from the corner stall."

Zainab *Khala*, Laila's mother, nodded with a smile.

"*Lablabu*? What's that?" asked Ariana as she wandered in and sat next to her mother.

"They're sugared beets," said Ariana's mother, Nasreen. "I loved eating them when I was little. They come in all sorts of colors and taste better than candy."

Sugared beets? I don't think so. Ariana shuddered. She glanced over at her elegantly dressed mother, with her chic haircut and tasteful choice of mauve lipstick. She couldn't imagine her standing on a dusty, noisy street eating from a dirty plate. Her mother was very particular about germs and scrubbed the kitchen counters twice a day.

"After Mother finished up her grocery shopping on Flower Street, if we had time, we'd go and get ice cream in Shahrenaw Park," said Laila, turning her back toward Ariana.

"Unfortunately, we couldn't go out that much anymore," said Zainab *Khala*. "It's just too dangerous."

"But if you let me, I'd spend hours at the Ka Farushi bird market," Laila said, smiling.

"Is that old place still around?" asked Hava Bibi.

"Oh, yes," replied Laila. "Father bought me a pair of songbirds there last year. They're just beautiful." She paused a moment with a frown. "I had to give them to Saima, my best friend, before we left."

"I'm sure Saima is taking great care of them," said Hava Bibi, patting Laila on the shoulder.

"Kabul has grown by leaps and bounds," said Zainab *Khala*, "war or no war. And the markets are filled with every kind of black market good you can think of—televisions, DVD players, silks, and fine china plates. But the poorest of the poor can barely afford bread."

The others sadly nodded while Ariana sat curled up against a cushion, feeling left out. They'd all lived in Kabul and had memories of their life there. She picked at the line of stitching across the toe of her old sock, hating the feel of it bunched up against her skin. Although her mother tried hard to find seamless clothes for her, including socks and underwear, sometimes it was not possible.

"Life was different in Afghanistan," said Hava Bibi with a sad smile. "It was a hard life, but also filled with fun times."

Zainab *Khala* and Laila exchanged a pensive glance. Catching their despondent look, Hava Bibi launched into another story. "Did I ever tell you the story about the feud?"

Hearing the word "feud," Ariana perked up. *Now, this sounds interesting.*

"No, Hava Bibi. Please tell us," urged Laila.

"Well, it's a story from our old village in the province Kunar, where our family originally comes from. It's quite beautiful—a lush, green valley nestled among the Hindu Kush Mountains. A wide river, shimmering like turquoise, runs through the middle, carrying the icy waters from the glaciers above."

"I've never been to Kunar but always wanted to go," said Laila.

"It isn't safe to travel there these days," said her mother in a subdued voice. "It's been overrun by the Taliban."

"I was nearly fifteen and had finished up my studies at the local school," continued Hava Bibi. "That's when the incident with the old goat occurred."

"A goat?" squeaked Ariana. She got a warning look from her mother not to interrupt.

But Laila keeps interrupting, Ariana thought, and bristled.

"Yes, *jaan*, a goat," said Hava Bibi, tweaking Ariana's nose. Ariana smiled; she and her grandmother were very close, especially since her grandfather, Masood *Baba*, had passed away four years before.

"Well, my father, Zia, owned a goat that had wandered onto our neighbor's land to eat some new spring grass. Now, my father was known in the village as a tough, ornery old man, and when the goat didn't return, he accused the neighbor, Bawer, of stealing it. Insulted that his *nang*, or honor, would be questioned in such a way, Bawer refused to return the mangy old goat. My father was infuriated and wanted *badal*, revenge. So in the middle of the night, he and my three brothers recaptured the goat, and in the process, to redeem their *nang*, they took Bawer's prized white stallion, the fastest in the valley."

"All that trouble for a goat?" said Ariana, her eyebrows arched.

"If the men had not been so hotheaded, the incident should have ended right there," said Hava Bibi. "Bawer's daughter, Dilshad, was my good friend at school, and before the feud began, our mothers often visited each other, exchanging melons and pomegranates from their orchards," she added with a melancholy look.

"So what happened?" Ariana asked with impatience.

"Yes, well, my father was known as—how do you kids say in American—'a real tough cookie.'"

Ariana giggled as her mother explained the saying to Laila and her mother.

"My father ruled the village with an iron fist, and after he took the stallion, things escalated. It was rumored that Bawer's eldest son burned down my father's apple orchard. Then my father retaliated by filling their well with sand. It went on like this for many years, leading eventually to my father shooting Bawer's son Tofan as he climbed over the mud boundary wall that separated our houses."

"He shot him?" Ariana said in a horrified whisper.

"Yes." Hava Bibi sighed, a look of disapproval on her elegant features. "It was stubbornness on both sides, really; Father spotted Tofan at the top of the wall and shouted to Bawer that if his son didn't get down, he would shoot. Bawer had told his son to climb the wall, so his *nang* was at stake. Tofan was an obedient Pukhtun son and would never question his father, so he stayed. Because Zia had given his word that he would shoot, he was stuck."

"His word? Are you kidding?" mumbled Ariana.

Laila gave her an incredulous look. "Ariana, giving your word is a big deal to Pukhtuns. In *Pukhtunwali* you are judged by your words and actions."

Ariana gave Laila a stony look. "I'm not stupid, okay?"

"Ariana," said her mother with a note of warning in her voice.

As Laila shifted her gaze, Ariana couldn't help but think that the only time Laila talked to her was to show off and make her look like an idiot.

"Don't be silly, Ariana *jaan*," said Hava Bibi. "You are not stupid. You just don't know about Afghan culture as much as Laila does. A Pukhtun man's worth is tied to his word. So my father, using a rusty old rifle left over by the British when they failed to conquer the Afghans, pulled the trigger."

"Did he die?" asked Laila's mother in a soft whisper.

"Thankfully, he did not," said Hava Bibi, a sad, wistful look on her face. "Tofan was hit in the leg and he fell. Dilshad and I stopped speaking after that, though I heard that Tofan went on to become a professor of literature at Kabul University."

"It's kind of like the Hatfields and McCoys," said Ariana, remembering what they'd learned in American history the year before.

"The who and who?" asked Hava Bibi.

"The Hatfields and McCoys were two families in West Virginia in the 1880s," explained Ariana. "A Hatfield shot and killed a McCoy, which started a family feud over honor that went on for decades."

"Yes, very similar," said Hava Bibi, her lips pressed in disapproval. Reliving the past had gotten her visibly upset. "Do you see how a small thing such as an argument over a goat can lead to something so terrible? If my father and Bawer had just met and talked things through, the families would still be friends."

"So how did it end?" asked Ariana.

"Fate had other plans," said Hava Bibi. "The feud simmered on and off for many years until the Soviets bombed our village after they invaded Afghanistan in 1979. Then both families scattered. I fled with my brothers, cousins, husband, and sons to neighboring Pakistan."

Ariana knew that her grandparents had eventually left Pakistan and ended up here, in Fremont, California, where many Afghans settled as refugees. Ariana's father, Jamil had been fourteen and Uncle Shams had been eleven when they'd arrived.

"Okay, kids, enough old stories," interrupted Nasreen. "School starts tomorrow, and we've got to get the rest of your school supplies."

Ariana reluctantly got up along with the others. While everyone else exited the living room, her mother pulled her aside.

"Ariana," said her mother, her face stern. "You were very rude to Laila, and that is not acceptable. She's your cousin, and our guest. You must be nice to her and make her feel welcome."

Reluctantly, Ariana nodded and trudged back to the garage to grab her school shopping list. The garage, her father's office, was overflowing with stuff related to the store. Cracking open the door, she glimpsed her father hunkered over his desk, poring over the store's ledgers and taking notes. Watching his worried face in the shadow cast by the lamp, Ariana felt her annoyance with Laila and her mother fizzle, replaced with a feeling of dread. Deep in her gut, she knew that the new store opening at the opposite end of the plaza was bad news.

3

School's In

BACK STRAIGHT, GAME FACE ON, Ariana pushed through the double doors of Brookhaven Middle School. One step behind was Laila, dressed in jeans she'd ironed that morning at six a.m., and a long, turquoise *kameez* she'd worn when she'd first arrived in San Francisco. After getting ready, as Ariana had dragged herself out of bed, Laila had helped Hava Bibi make breakfast, gaining praise for flipping a perfect pancake. She'd even added mini chocolate chips for the twins, earning her a rare hug from Omar.

Pretending her cousin wasn't there, Ariana halted under the cheerful green and white banner welcoming everyone back to school. *Where's Mariam? I'm going to kill her if she's late.* They'd promised to meet in the lobby then check bulletin boards to see their homeroom assignment so they could officially begin the sixth grade together. Over the summer they'd attended middle school orientation and received a map of the school, along with instruction on what to expect this year.

"There are so many people," whispered Laila, her face pale.

Ariana nodded, still irritated by Laila's kissing up to her annoying brothers. But her mother's voice reverberated in the back of her head. *Keep an eye on Laila. She's new, and I'm sure things will be a little scary for her.* "Yeah," replied Ariana, feeling a little overwhelmed too. "There are more than six hundred students here."

"Oh," murmured Laila, rubbing her locket.

A stream of kids came bobbing through the main door, and Ariana began to wish she were back at Glenmoor Elementary, with its comforting yellow walls, folksy art hanging from the bulletin boards, the familiar teachers, and the cozy cafeteria that looked out onto the playground. Feeling anxious, she wiggled her toes in her new seamless stockings that her mother had bought from a special store on the Internet. To make the first day of school go by more easily, she'd also dressed in her most comfortable clothes. There was no way that she wanted to be noticed yanking at underwear that bunched up or a shirt seam that dug into her skin. When Ariana was six, Nasreen had taken her to the pediatrician, fed up with tantrums about clothes that didn't feel right, were too tight, or itched. Ariana had been diagnosed with a mild case of Sensory Processing Disorder; she tended to feel, smell, and hear things at a heightened level. Ariana wasn't too bothered by it—that was just the way she was. But she knew her mother had been disappointed; Nasreen had loved buying her only daughter fancy outfits, adorned with bows, lace, and ruffles, and dressing her up. After the trip to the doctor, all that had ended.

"And there are so many . . . boys . . . ," added Laila, her voice subdued.

Ariana blinked in surprise, realizing how weird that must have been for her, coming from an all-girls school. "Don't worry about them," she said. "They're just . . . people. Sometimes kind of loud and gross, like my brothers, but they're okay."

Laila nodded, edging closer as a backpack came flying past. Ariana combed through the sea of bodies and spotted a few familiar faces, including Selena Ramirez and George Kakopolis, who shared a friendly wave. It was a relief to see them, but it was still daunting to start out in an unfamiliar building with unknown kids and teachers.

"Hey, Ari!" came Mariam's melodious voice from across the hall. A good half a head shorter than everyone else, she made her way through the throng of bodies, wearing a bright pink top, white jeans, and a leather headband holding back long hair the color of dark honey. She moved through the hall, as comfortable as could be. For a moment Ariana felt jealous of her best friend's outgoing, can-do personality. Nothing ever seemed to faze her.

"Hey, Mariam," said Ariana, breathing a sigh of relief.

"Hey to you, too," said Mariam. "*Salaam*, Laila. How are you doing?"

Laila grimaced, her lips compressed.

"Don't worry," said Mariam, giving Laila a hug. "I remember coming from Afghanistan and starting school for the first time. It was really scary, but it all turned out okay. We're here to help you. Right, Ari?"

"Yeah," mumbled Ariana without much enthusiasm.

"This is a beautiful school—," said Laila, staring at the freshly painted white walls.

"It's okay—could be better," said Ariana, cutting her off. "The gym is kind of small, and the cafeteria doesn't have windows. I wish we had a bigger library and a pool."

"Lycée Malalai, my old school, had bullet holes in the walls and half of it was demolished during the bombings," said Laila.

Bullet holes? Ariana blinked in surprise.

"Wow," said Mariam. "That's awful."

Ariana knew that the Taliban had stopped girls from going to school, but she thought things had gotten better since they'd been forced out. Then she remembered her father and Uncle Shams's conversation at the store. *The Taliban are gaining in strength . . .* Maybe having a small gym and library wasn't such a bad thing after all.

"Come on. We need to get our homeroom assignment," said Mariam.

They wove their way through the press of bodies to the bulletin board outside the school office. A handful of teachers stood by to help. The girls pored over the first sheet, looking for their names. None were there, so they moved on to the next.

"Here I am," squealed Mariam, pointing at the list for 6B.

"Let me see," said Ariana, pushing Laila out of the way. She'd been in the same class with Mariam since the second grade, and they'd been praying that they'd end up in the same homeroom. After seeing Mariam's name in the first column, she kept reading, but there was no "Ariana Shinwari." Halfway through the second row her hope started to fade. But there, at the end of the list, she caught the name Shinwari. But it wasn't her; it was Laila. Disappointment left a bitter taste in her mouth. *How can this happen?*

"Hey, we're in the same homeroom," said Mariam, grabbing a relieved-looking Laila's hand.

"I'm not here," said Ariana with a strangled whisper.

"Don't worry," said Mariam, looking hopeful. "I'm sure we'll have other classes together. Homeroom lasts only half an hour anyway."

"Come along, guys," said a tall, balding teacher in crisp khakis and a peach button-down shirt. "If you know your homeroom assignment, hurry along. The bell's going to ring any minute."

"I guess we have to go," said Mariam. "We'll see you later." She grabbed Laila's hand, and they disappeared into the crush.

With a frustrated sigh Ariana checked the other lists and found that she was in 6D. Hitching up her backpack, she trudged to her assigned room. She made her way to the third row, in the middle of room, and sat down. It was the perfect spot to hear the teacher, but not so far in front that she'd get called on all the time.

"Hey, Ari," said Selena, grabbing the desk next to her.

"Hey, how was your summer?" replied Ariana, relieved to see her.

"Pretty good. We went down to Bakersfield to spend a few weeks on my grandparents' almond farm. Man, it's *so* hot down there."

As Ariana nodded, a tiny woman with bright red hair and glasses bounded inside. With a flourish she wrote her name on the blackboard. "Good morning. I'm Ms. Van Buren, and I'll be your homeroom teacher this year. I know a lot of you might be nervous, starting at a new school, seeing so many unfamiliar faces, but in homeroom our goal is to get to know one another better and prepare for a fantastic future in middle school. The first thing I'll do is take roll; so after I call your name, stand up, say something unique about yourself, and I'll give you your class schedule."

Groans and eye rolling followed her announcement. No one wanted to stand up in class and actually say something. Ms. Van Buren ignored the lack of enthusiasm and pulled out a manila envelope. "Okay, here I go. Melanie Aleve," she called out.

Melanie stood up and took a deep breath. She told the class in a rush of words that she loved to ice skate and hoped to be like Kristi Yamaguchi, an Olympic figure skater from Fremont. Ariana gave Melanie props for being first, and waited for her name to be called, racking her brains for something interesting to say. After Roger Chu, Ms. Van Buren called on Gopal Ganguly, who played the tabla, Indian drums. Ariana recognized him from Glenmoor Elementary. After him came Wali Ghilzai, who stood up with lazy confidence. As his chocolate-brown eyes collided with hers, he told the class he'd recently moved to Fremont from Los Angeles and that he liked to skateboard.

How boring is that? thought Ariana, glancing away. When it was her turn, she stood up and told the class about her love of origami and how she was working on a menagerie of zoo animals. As she sat back down, she sensed a pair of eyes staring at her. It was Wali, looking at her with odd intensity. *What a weirdo,* she thought. She gave him a questioning look and glanced away, her nose in the air.

Ariana got home from school at 3:14, sweaty, exhausted, and grumpy. She shrugged off her backpack and spotted Zayd in the dining room, doing his homework. Obviously the high school teachers had not been easy on the first day, and he was immersed in a calculus book, a look of intense concentration straining his face. He'd be applying to college next year, along with Fadi, whose sister Noor had set the bar high by getting into UC Berkeley and was applying to medical school. After having visited the sprawling campus earlier in the summer, Zayd was dead set on getting into UC Berkeley's school of engineering, and Ariana knew her parents had high expectations of him. They'd been monitoring his grades all during high school so that he didn't slip up.

In the kitchen, Ariana grabbed a stack of sandwich cookies and a glass of milk, and headed to the garage. The twins would be home any minute, and she wanted to disappear before then. She knew that even after an hour of rigorous soccer practice, they'd come in like a tornado. Her mother swore that if she figured out how to bottle their boisterous energy, the family would be millionaires.

Thankfully, she hadn't gotten any homework and

had somehow managed to navigate the confusing halls of Brookhaven without getting lost more than twice. Both times she'd made it to class just as the bell had rung, though she'd been a little out of breath. After homeroom she, Mariam, and Laila had run into one another on the way to math, which they all had together. When Ariana and Mariam had compared their schedules, it had turned out that they had only one other class together—art, two days a week.

"This stinks," Ariana had muttered, gripping her schedule in her fist.

"It's okay," said Mariam, patting her on the shoulder. "We've got the same lunch period, every day."

Ariana shrugged and shoved the miserable schedule into her backpack, catching a glimpse of Laila, who was standing next to Mariam, hugging her schedule to her chest, as silent as a ghost once again.

"How are your classes?" Ariana asked grudgingly, remembering her mother's words to be nice.

"Pretty good," murmured Laila, glancing at Mariam with a smile.

"Yeah," said Mariam with a grin. "Laila and I actually ended up having language arts, science, and PE together."

"*What?*" said Ariana. "Let me see."

Laila reluctantly handed over her schedule, and Ariana pored over the list. Mariam was wrong. They also had math together, with her. So they practically shared *all* the same classes. She felt like she'd been hit in the stomach by a ton of bricks.

"But, hey, guess what I found out," said Mariam, her hazel eyes crinkled with joy.

"What?" grumbled Ariana.

"I ran into the president of the drama club putting up a sign on the bulletin board," said Mariam. "They're holding tryouts next week."

"Really?" said Ariana, perking up a little.

"Yeah, and the play this year is *Peter Pan*."

"You're definitely going to get a lead part," said Ariana, momentarily forgetting the awful schedule.

"Yeah, and you're going to design an awesome set," said Mariam. "You're so artistic. And maybe Laila can help you."

Ariana nodded without much enthusiasm, feeling as if some unforeseen force were trying to ruin her life. She sat mute for the rest of the day. Conflicting thoughts raged through her head. *Is Laila out to steal my best friend?* It didn't really make sense, Ariana knew, but it sure felt that way. *What if Mariam ends up liking the perfect Laila more than she likes me?* She'd watched the two of them walk away, heads bowed toward each other, long hair flowing behind them, speaking in Pukhto, laughing over a story of what it was like to go to school in Afghanistan, something Ariana had never done. They seemed like a perfect pair, and she was the imperfect odd man out.

Ariana now flipped on the garage lights that her father had installed, to cast a warm glow over the carpeted interior. Tucked away next to a bookshelf sat her treasured plastic storage box. Her father had gotten it for her to hold her origami "stuff"—the stack of beautiful textured paper of varying materials, thicknesses, and styles; her origami guidebook; two pairs of scissors; tape; glue; a ruler; and calculator. Above the box hung her Peanuts calendar, and she took a red pen and drew a satisfying *X* on today's date. One day closer to moving into their new house. *And my new room.*

She filled her lungs with a deep, calming breath and laid out supplies on her father's desk. Gently she removed a sheet of nubby gray-and-silver *chiyogami*, a type of *washi* paper featuring woodblock-printed designs. Next she cut out a dollar-size portion of paper and set it in front of her. She grabbed her guidebook and opened it to the page on elephants and read through the instructions, munching on a cookie.

Slowly the tension eased from her shoulders and she was ready to work.

She adjusted the paper so that the wide side faced her, and she made a horizontal valley fold at the half-way point of the sheet, as well as at the top corners, as if making a paper airplane. Biting the inside of her cheek in concentration, she folded the right edge of the paper back until it was doubled. She was about to make the next fold when she heard footsteps outside the garage door and froze in the middle of making a crease.

"Shams, what did you find out?" came her father's muffled voice through the garage door.

Ariana hesitated, uncertain what to do. Should she go back into the house? But they'd probably hear the door open. She didn't want to be caught eavesdropping again. But she wasn't trying to snoop—she was just sitting there, minding her own business.

Uncle Shams cleared his throat. "A friend told me to go see Ronald Hammersmith. He's a real estate developer and sits on the city's zoning board. He's also running for mayor."

"Yes, well, what did he say?" pushed Jamil.

"I explained our situation to him," said Uncle Shams. "He was helpful and very sympathetic; he said it would be tough having a similar business open next to ours. But unfortunately, our lease does not have a non-compete clause—meaning Lucinda can rent to a competing store if she wants to. He said if we'd built in a non-compete, she wouldn't have been able to lease to a similar store."

"That's what I was afraid of," said Jamil, his voice weary. "When we first took out the lease, we had no idea we needed such a clause."

"That's not all," said Uncle Shams. "I was at the mosque for evening prayers earlier today and found out the name of the new store's owners."

"Who are they?"

"A guy who just moved into town a few months ago," said Uncle Shams. "Gulbadin Ghilzai."

"Why does that name sound familiar?" pondered Jamil, as Uncle Shams continued talking.

But Ariana was no longer listening to either of them. Her breath caught in her throat as she remembered a set of chocolate-brown eyes from homeroom, the ones belonging to Wali Ghilzai.

4

Grand Opening

FROM KABUL CORNER'S FRONT window Ariana had a prime spot for viewing the grand opening festivities over at Pamir Market. Even though their official opening had been the day before, from the looks of things the celebration raged on. Faint hints of music floated in from the troupe of Afghan musicians entertaining the crowd gathered outside Pamir Market. Green and white balloons floated above, their strings intertwined with golden streamers glinting in the sun. Ariana slouched against the glass, watching customers, many she recognized as regulars at their store, weave past the musicians, laden with groceries.

She spotted Wali working the crowd, platter in hand, passing out free almond cookies.

At least she no longer had to keep her lips zipped about the new store—the Ghilzais had taken out an ad on the Afghan radio station, announcing their grand opening. Sara *Khala* had heard the ad and had bustled over, a whirlwind in tangerine stripes, with Uncle Shams in tow, and they had disappeared into the garage with Ariana's parents. The adults had stayed behind closed doors for a while and had emerged looking tired and more than a little worried. Soon after, gossip had begun bubbling about the new store. People in the Afghan community wondered how the Shinwari brothers were dealing with the competition. Some felt that Kabul Corner had been a monopoly for too long, controlling prices of Afghan groceries.

Ariana leaned back with a sigh. It seemed like Kabul Corner had had only half its usual customers come in that weekend. Her father sat behind the counter, a frown furrowing his brows as he watched the television hanging from the opposite wall. It was locked on an Afghan channel, broadcasting coverage from across the Atlantic. Usually customers would linger, grab a cup of tea, and chat with her father and uncle about recent happenings. But today the store was pretty quiet. The customers who did come were just there for the bread, which always sold out. Besides Ariana and her father, the only others in the store were Laila, who was sweeping out the back, the baker, the butcher, and a handful of loyal customers who'd sworn they'd never step into the new store.

"So, brother Jamil, it looks like quite a circus over there," said Mrs. Balkh, her white hair pulled back beneath her turquoise scarf.

"Yes." Jamil smiled graciously. "It's understandable. A new store is exciting."

Mr. Balkh harrumphed, leaning on his cane. "All those musicians and decorations look suspicious to me. It makes me wonder what they're trying to hide."

Ariana giggled. Mr. Balkh had been a police chief in Afghanistan, and he viewed everyone with suspicion.

"I agree," said Soraiya Khanum, coming up the aisle with a basket of groceries. "Tried and true, I say—Kabul Corner is the only store for me."

"I will only shop in your store," added Mrs. Balkh. "I was the first person here ten years ago and will be the last!"

As Ariana's father thanked Mrs. Balkh, she asked for a box of tea, which she'd forgotten.

"Laila," called out Jamil, "please bring up a box of the superfine green tea."

"*Salaam,*" said Laila, running up and handing Mrs. Balkh the box.

"My, what a lovely young girl," said the elderly woman, adjusting the spectacles on her thin nose.

"This is my niece Laila," said Jamil. "She just arrived from Afghanistan a month ago."

Soraiya Khanum and Mrs. Balkh spoke to Laila in Farsi, marveling at her gracious manners.

"Laila is very talented," said Jamil. "You should hear her recite poetry—"

"Recite one for us, my dear," interrupted Mr. Balkh, his craggy features softening.

Laila cleared her throat, looking a bit uncomfortable. But she launched into a melodious recitation of a fairly long poem in Farsi.

Ariana stood by, not understanding a word of it.

"Oh my, how clever," gushed Soraiya Khanum. She looked over and spotted Ariana. "Don't you think so, my dear?"

"Oh, Ariana doesn't speak Farsi," said Jamil.

Ariana's ears burned as Laila looked away.

"Oh," said Soraiya Khanum, looking disappointed.

"Well, I'm sure there must be an English translation of the Rumi poem," said Mrs. Balkh. "It's about shadow and light. It's just beautiful."

Ariana nodded, feeling invisible and inconsequential. She went back to stacking the chips as the trio purchased their groceries and left.

"The others will be back," Jamil told Ariana, catching her looking out the window later that day. "Pamir Market is new and exciting, but we have excellent products and unparalleled customer service. Plus, they don't have a bakery, and our bread is the best in town—soft on the inside, crisp on the outside, and hot right out of the oven."

Ariana nodded, returning to her chores. She picked up a stack of cardboard boxes and headed to the back, passing the small bakery. Haroon, their baker, was pulling out the last load of bread for the day. Most of the thin loaves, nearly three feet in length, had been sold as soon as they'd come out of the oven that morning. Afghans were very particular about their *doday*, or "bread." The word "*doday*" itself meant not only "bread" but "food," since meals were so hard to come by in poverty-stricken, war-torn Afghanistan. Many families subsisted on bread and salt, and were happy enough to have even that.

Inhaling the warm, inviting yeasty smell, Ariana felt proud that they had the best bread in Fremont. The old customers that had shown up that day had grabbed a stack of fresh bread, and then had scurried over to check out the new store. Her father was right; Pamir Market was just new and shiny and would be old news soon enough. And all their customers would be back, since they still came in for their bread anyway. She skirted past the bakery, careful not to disturb Haroon, as he was notoriously temperamental. She still winced from the yelling fit he'd given the kids for getting in his way. Actually, he didn't much like anyone, but he got along with Musa, the butcher, but that was only because they had made a deal to stay out of each other's way. With a sigh Ariana passed Laila and pretended she didn't see her.

It was noisy as usual at Uncle Shams's house as Ariana laid a steaming platter of rice on the *dastarkhan*, a long table cloth laid out on the ground, where everyone sat to eat their meals. Laila placed a bowl of stew next to the pile of bread in the middle, from Kabul Corner, of course. She stopped to playfully ruffle Hasan's hair as he stole a piece of bread and the family crowded together, grabbing their customary spots. Laila now sat in Ariana's favorite position, next to Hava Bibi, while Ariana had been shunted over to sit with Uncle Shams's younger boys, Marjan and Taroon, who at eight and six thought it was hilarious to stick carrot sticks into their ears. Gritting her teeth, Ariana elbowed her way between them and plopped down. Her uncle, usually full of news from around the neighborhood, was uncharacteristically quiet as he settled down next to his wife with a long, breathy sigh.

"What's wrong?" asked Hava Bibi, passing Uncle Shams the salad bowl.

"Nothing to worry about, Mom," said Jamil, giving his brother a look that said, *Don't worry her.* "There were some missing deliveries at the store. That's all."

Ariana leaned closer, trying to hear what the grown-ups were saying, over the boys' snorts about some dumb joke.

"Yeah," mumbled Uncle Shams. "Nothing to worry about."

"Is it about this new store?" asked Hava Bibi, her eyes narrowed. "I do know things, even though I don't leave the house much."

Ariana smiled. Her grandmother *did* seem to know everything. She had her ways—dozens of other grandmothers and aunties who got on the phone and passed along the news, local and international.

"No, no," said Uncle Shams, vigorously shaking his head, digging into the salad with unusual enthusiasm.

"Now, Shams," said Hava Bibi. "I've known you all your life, and I know when something is worrying you."

Uncle Shams stabbed a piece of lettuce, and his resolve to stay quiet dissolved at Hava Bibi's persistence. "Yes, Mother," he burst out. "It's that darn new store that's bothering me. It's ruining our business!"

"Shams," exclaimed his wife, Sara *Khala*. "Watch your language—the kids!"

Uncle Shams's cheeks reddened, and the boys snickered till Sara *Khala* turned and gave them the *look*. Sara *Khala*, with a love of bright colors and loud prints, was plump like her husband and usually had a sweet disposition. But when she got mad, the kids got in line.

"It's ruining your business?" said Hava Bibi, blinking in surprise. "What do you mean, *ruin*? What are they *doing*?"

"Now, hold on," said Jamil, shooting his brother an annoyed look. "Don't blow things out of proportion and worry everyone." Uncle Shams averted his gaze and shoveled cherry tomatoes into his mouth as Jamil continued. "The new store may give us some competition, but they're not really *doing* anything to us."

Uncle Shams muttered, "As if choosing a location right across from us on Wong Plaza isn't *doing* anything."

"Look," Jamil said, sighing, "it's not an ideal situation, but there's enough business for both of us."

Ariana saw that her grandmother could sense an argument brewing between her sons. *Time to change the subject.* "If you work hard, Allah provides," she said soothingly as she lifted the large tray of rice.

"Yes, *insha'*Allah, it will be all right," said Jamil.

But Uncle Shams couldn't help but have the last word. "It'll be all right as long as those Ghilzais don't do anything tricky."

"What did you say?" asked Hava Bibi, her cheeks turning pale.

"About what?" said Uncle Shams.

"What *name* did you say?" repeated Hava Bibi, confusion clouding her eyes.

Uncle Shams frowned. "The new owner is named Ghilzai—Gulbadin Ghilzai. Oh, there's an old uncle, too. Tofan."

Hava Bibi's hand shook, and as if in slow motion,

the tray slipped, sending white grains flying. All conversation stopped. Even the boys paused midchew.

"Bibi, are you all right?" asked Ariana's mom, getting up to help the older woman.

"Oh my goodness," whispered Hava Bibi, slumping against the cushions.

"What is it, Mom?" asked Jamil.

"Remember the old story?" said Hava Bibi, looking agitated.

Ariana had leaned so far over the *dastarkhan* that her elbow was practically in the meatball stew. She had *never* seen Hava Bibi look flustered, not even when a car had hit Omar in front of the house. Her grandmother had flown into action and stopped the bleeding on his head while waiting for the ambulance to arrive. That was the incident that had left him with the scar that cut across his eyebrow.

"Which story?" asked Sara *Khala*.

"The one about the goat!" cried Hava Bibi.

"I have a vague recollection of some such story," Jamil said, picking up the rice that had flown into his lap.

"The old family feud, the one that started when our ornery old goat wandered onto our neighbor's land— the neighbor was *Bawer Ghilzai*!"

"Do you think it's those Ghilzais?" said Uncle

Shams, coughing as he swallowed a mouthful of lettuce.

Hava Bibi sat back, her face drawn. "Tofan Ghilzai was my friend, Dilshad's, brother. The feud that started over the goat ended with my father, Zia, shooting him!"

The entire story came flooding through Ariana's brain, and she rocked back on her heels.

"The shooting happened before you were born," said Hava Bibi, twisting her hands into her scarf. "After that our families settled into an uncomfortable truce, but eventually war with the Soviets began and our village was bombed by Russian jets. All the families fled, and we ended up here."

"So why are they here, opening a store in the same shopping complex as us?" said Uncle Shams, suspicion contorting his features.

"It's probably just a coincidence," said Jamil.

"Coincidence?" said Uncle Shams, suddenly alert. "Somehow I don't think so."

"Now, Shams," said Hava Bibi, regaining her composure. "Jamil is probably right. Tofan and his nephew probably don't even know who we are. Shinwari is a common clan name."

Uncle Shams sat back, hands folded across his ample

belly, unconvinced. "This can't possibly be a coincidence."

"Shams, you're getting worked up again," warned Jamil.

"No, really," said Shams. "Why else would they open a store at the opposite end of Wong Plaza from us? I bet they're continuing the feud and want *badal*, for Grandfather Zia shooting Tofan. They want to drive us out of business!"

"Shams," said Hava Bibi, her voice tense. "I want no talk of the *feud* and *badal*. As far as I'm concerned, the feud ended when we all left Afghanistan. You and Jamil should go over and introduce yourselves, show there are no hard feelings."

"But, Mom—," muttered Shams.

"Shush!" said Hava Bibi. "It was a silly goat, and the feud is over. Swear to me you will not even think such nonsense!"

"All right," grumbled Shams.

"Mom *is* right," said Jamil, though there was a hint of doubt in his eyes. "Maybe we'll go around tomorrow and welcome them to the plaza."

"If you say so," said Shams, pushing aside the salad on his plate and piling on chicken kebob.

"Look, we just have to work harder to get customers excited and back at the store," said Jamil. "Maybe a new advertisement or a raffle or something."

As Ariana listened to her father about the cost of radio ads and flyers, something dense settled at the bottom of her stomach; apprehension combined with growing anger. *The news keeps getting worse.*

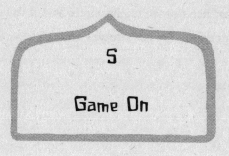

5

Game On

ARIANA'S MIND WANDERED DURING Mr. Lambert's discussion on the importance of habitat conservation, and she rubbed the back of her neck where her mother had removed the chenille shirt's tag. The rough line of the label scratched her skin, driving her to distraction. She gritted her teeth, trying to focus on the picture of a squat, ugly European green crab Mr. Lambert held up. He was explaining how the crustaceans had found their way into the San Francisco Bay by stowing away in the ballast water of visiting cargo ships. The voracious invader species had killed off ninety percent of the native shore crabs and threatened them with extinction. It reminded her of Uncle Shams's dire warning that the opening of a new store would drive the Shinwaris out of business. Kabul Corner was an endangered species, and Pamir Market was their chief predator. Even though Hava Bibi and Ariana's father had calmed everyone down and convinced them that the Ghilzais were not out to drive the store out of business, anxiety hung over the Shinwari home. Everyone felt it.

Two weeks had passed since Pamir Market's grand opening, but the buzz surrounding the store hadn't died down, and the number of customers shopping at Kabul Corner had been cut by more than half. Well, except for their bread. Everyone still came to get bread from them, but then disappeared across the plaza to buy the rest of their groceries at Pamir Market. Mr. Balkh had gone in as a spy and reported back that the Ghilzais had marked down all their groceries by ten cents in comparison to Kabul Corner. If you added that up, people shopping at Pamir Market were saving at least five to fifteen dollars a visit. *With savings like that, why would they ever come back?*

Pressure built within Ariana's chest, like a volcano building up magma. *Why did the Ghilzais have to open a store so close to Kabul Corner? Why couldn't they have gone somewhere else?* Her father had run into Gulbadin in the parking lot earlier that week and introduced himself. Later that afternoon, over lunch, he'd told Hava Bibi that he'd done his duty to be hospitable and welcomed the Ghilzais to the plaza, but since Gulbadin had been in a hurry, they hadn't talked much. In the back of her mind, even though her grandmother insisted that the feud had ended back in Afghanistan, Ariana couldn't help but wonder if the Ghilzais had *really* gotten over the old feud.

The bell rang, interrupting Ariana's worried thoughts. She tugged on her shirt and trudged out, relieved that lunch was next. Caught up in the rush of students, Ariana navigated toward her slightly dented locker. After tossing her books inside, she grabbed her lunch box and slammed the door shut. The loud clang made her feel slightly better, so she gave her locker a whack for good measure. Down the hall she spotted Mariam's tawny head, close to Laila's, bobbing through the crowd. Ariana knew they'd just had social studies and were working on their ancient Egypt project together. The pressure in her midsection pushed against her heart. *It's so not fair. Perfect Laila gets to work with Mariam, and I'm stuck with knuckleheaded Josh.*

Since Ariana hadn't known anyone well enough in her social studies class, the teacher had randomly put together the remaining kids who hadn't found partners. In her case it had been a slouchy towheaded boy named Josh Scrimption; he'd looked as thrilled to be with her as she had been to be paired up with him. So far Josh had vetoed everything she'd suggested. He even hated her idea of making a model of Pharaoh Cheops's royal barge. *It should have been me working with Mariam to mummify beetles, not Laila.* Ariana's fingers tightened around the metal handle of her lunch box. It seemed like she hadn't seen Mariam in more than a week—not after school, or during it either. Laila, on the other hand, was attached to her best friend's hip with superglue.

"Hey, Ari," called out Mariam. "Ready for lunch?"

Ariana nodded, releasing her death grip on her lunch box.

"How was Mr. Lambert's class?" asked Mariam. A thick sheen of pink lip gloss stained her lips.

"Eh," mumbled Ariana. "It was okay."

"You okay? You look kind of tense," said Mariam with a frown.

"I'm fine," muttered Ariana.

"What's going on over there?" interrupted Laila,

pointing to a gaggle of kids surrounding a table at the end of the hall.

"Oooh, let's see," said Mariam. "Maybe it's a bake sale."

The thought of freshly baked cookies perked Ariana up. Maybe they'd have her favorite—snickerdoodles, covered in a thick coating of cinnamon sugar.

The trio edged closer, and from where she stood Ariana spotted a familiar girl sitting at the edge of the table—Patty Marsh, one of the popular girls from Ariana's old elementary school. Patty was also the current editor of the Brookhaven newspaper, *The Owl*. Next to her sat her second in command, Yoojin, a large box in front of her. Ariana's enthusiasm deflated. *No baked goods*. The crush of bodies propelled them toward a gap at the front of the table. Up close Ariana saw that the box was plastered with pictures of kids—poor, sad-looking kids. The label across the top read BROOKHAVEN KIDS HELPING KIDS IN NEED. But it was the person sitting next to Yoojin who gripped Ariana's attention. It was Wali, wearing a bright yellow-and-purple Los Angeles Lakers T-shirt, smiling, and handing out flyers.

"How's it going, Patty, Wali?" came a familiar adult voice from behind them.

"Great, Principal Chiu," bubbled Patty, popping up like a yo-yo. "Thanks for introducing me to Wali. He's fund-raised for orphans before, and he totally knows what he's doing."

"Wonderful," said Principal Chiu, pausing at the table. "I knew you'd make a great team. Helping those in need is an important mission for the school this year."

Ariana recalled Principal Chiu's welcoming address on the first day of school. She'd announced that one of the school's initiatives this year was to raise money for the Kids in Need Program, which helped educate children from disadvantaged backgrounds. It was no surprise that a busybody like Patty had pushed her way into a leadership role, but seeing Wali next to her, as if he belonged, made Ariana feel like her head was going to explode.

"Are you *really* okay?" whispered Mariam. "You're kind of turning purple."

"I'm fine," growled Ariana, not recognizing her own voice.

"Hey, Wali," shouted a lanky boy as he entered the cafeteria. "See you at the court after school."

"Later," Wali answered with a wave.

"Wow. He seems to know everyone," whispered Laila.

Ariana glowered. "Just like his family, pushing their way in where they're not wanted."

"It doesn't look like he's not wanted," said Laila under her breath.

Ariana shot Laila a look that would have sizzled a steak. "Whose side are you on?"

"Don't be silly, Ari," said Mariam as Principal Chiu left. "Laila's your cousin; of course she's on your side."

Laila shot Mariam a grateful smile. Ariana stared at them, a sharp prick of hurt nicking her heart.

"Do you guys want one?" asked a hesitant voice.

Ariana tensed. She jerked her head back toward Wali, who'd extended a flyer toward her. Without thinking, she grabbed it, and then tore it up, the smooth lavender paper crumpling between her fingers. *That feels good.*

"Hey, what are you doing?" Patty said with a gasp as she and Yoojin looked on with horror.

"I don't want anything from *you*," growled Ariana. All of a sudden the image of a squat, beady-eyed European green crab flashed before her, threatening the local species.

Wali reddened and snatched his hand back.

"And we don't want your family around here either, so go back to stinking Los Angeles," added Ariana, throwing the fragments of paper at him. Then she stopped in disbelief. *That wasn't supposed to come out of my mouth.*

The kids around the table, who'd been jabbering away a second ago, went dead silent. Everyone was looking at Ariana like she'd sprouted horns on her head.

"Dude, what's wrong with you?" muttered a voice in the back.

"How dare you!" huffed Patty. "We're doing this to, like, help kids in need."

"She's, like, a total Grinch," sputtered Yoojin.

"Uh, she's been under a lot of stress," said Mariam loudly, grabbing Ariana's arm. "Really, really rough quiz in science . . ."

"Yes, very tough quiz," piped in Laila, her eyes wide at Ariana's odd behavior.

As Mariam pulled Ariana away, Wali whispered for her ears only. "We aren't going anywhere," he said. "This is a free country, and we're here to stay, whether *you* like it or not."

Ariana followed her nose into the kitchen and found Hava Bibi covered in a fine sprinkling of flour, kneading dough. She was making *gunzakhil*, a fried cookie, and the air smelled sweet with a hint of cardamom. The mouthwatering aroma sent a wave of comfort through Ariana. The day hadn't gotten any better when she'd arrived home from school. Mariam had just called, and not for her—for Laila. Ariana had thrust the phone into her cousin's hand and stomped toward the kitchen.

"*Salaam,* Ariana *jaan.* How was school?"

Ariana shrugged "Okay, I guess," she mumbled as she grabbed a golden cookie, still hot from the oil.

"Well, you don't look like it was okay," said Hava Bibi with a raised eyebrow.

Ariana sighed, cramming the cookie into her mouth. She knew her grandmother wasn't going to let her go without an explanation. "I ran into Wali at school," she said, swallowing. "Wali *Ghilzai.*"

"Oh?" said Hava Bibi, looking up as she rolled out cookies.

"Yeah, and we kind of exchanged some words."

"What kind of *words?*"

"I told him that he and his stinking family should go back to Los Angeles," mumbled Ariana, her cheeks reddening.

Hava Bibi sighed. "I understand your feelings, *jaan.* Your father and Shams have had the great fortune of owning the only Afghan grocery store in town. But a little bit of competition may be a good thing. It will challenge them to do better."

"But the Ghilzais had no right to open a store right *next* to us!"

"Perhaps the location is not the best, but they have every right to run any kind of business they want."

"But what if they're here because of the feud," muttered Ariana, the question burrowing its way out of her.

Hava Bibi waved the rolling pin at Ariana in an unexpected show of annoyance. "Don't even think that. That feud was left behind in Afghanistan with the death of my father and Bawer. I know Tofan, Gulbadin's uncle. He would never continue the feud . . ." Her voice went quiet. "He's a very honorable man."

Ariana nodded, chastised.

"So don't pick a fight with Wali. He had nothing to do with his family's decision."

"But he was, like, throwing it in my face," said Ariana, not able to stop herself.

"Really? He was rude to you?"

Ariana remembered that all Wali had done was offer her a flyer. He hadn't said anything obnoxious. It was she who'd done that.

"All I'm saying, my dear, is that you should not judge someone so quickly. Give him a chance. Remember, a Pukhtun must always be *imandar*.

"What does that mean?"

"It means 'righteous.' No matter how difficult a situation you find yourself in, you must try to have good thoughts, speak good words, and perform good deeds."

"I'll try, Bibi," mumbled Ariana. *But it's going to be really hard.*

"Ariana *jaan*, come help me with these," Jamil called as he entered the kitchen, with a large box from Krishna Kopymat in tow.

Ariana looked inside and saw huge stacks of advertisements printed on standard pale blue economy paper.

"I thought you could fold them up, since you like doing those paper foldy thingies," teased her father.

"It's called origami, dad," grumbled Ariana as she pulled out a light, almost translucent page and read the headline: FREE BREAD WITH PURCHASE OF $25 WORTH OF GROCERIES.

"These flyers should remind our old customers that since our bread is the best in town, they should get their groceries at Kabul Corner as well. We'll post them at the mosques and the community center, and advertise on the Afghan radio station."

"Do you think giving away free bread is a good idea?" asked Ariana.

"Oh, yes," said Jamil. "Your uncle and I talked it over. You know that we charge two-fifty per loaf of bread, but it only costs us one dollar to make. So we're really giving away a dollar's worth of stuff, but customers don't know that. They think they're getting something valuable—a loaf of our amazing bread." Jamil smiled, pleased with himself.

"It's a good idea," said Hava Bibi as Jamil returned to the garage.

Ariana nodded, realizing that it was a pretty brilliant move. She washed her hands and took out a stack of flimsy flyers and began folding while Hava Bibi hummed and fried cookies. A sense of confidence settled over Ariana; the game was on, and if the Ghilzais wanted to try to beat them, they were going to get a darn good fight. As the pile of papers grew, she heard a stampede heading toward the kitchen. The boys were back from soccer practice.

"*Salaam,* Bibi," chorused Omar and Hasan, followed by Baz, Marjan, and Taroon. They gave their grandmother a kiss and fell on the cookies.

"Boys," ordered Hava Bibi, "get some plates."

"Hey, watch out," grumbled Ariana, shaking away oily crumbs. She wrinkled her nose, disgusted as they chewed with their mouths open and slurped milk like a herd of hippopotamuses.

Hava Bibi shooed them into the dining room, giving Ariana some peace to work. But she'd already blocked them out, her mind swirling with delightful thoughts about how she was going to decorate her room at the new house. Just that morning she'd made another red *X* on her calendar. She smiled, debating what color to paint the walls. She dredged up the names of paint colors she'd seen at The Home Depot the week before, when she'd picked up supplies with her father. Lemon Grass, Sassy Blue, Honeysuckle, or even a shade of purple, like Vigorous Violet. Or maybe she'd use a textured wallpaper instead. . . .

6

Best Friends

FOR THE NEXT TWO weeks, to everyone's relief, Kabul Corner was flooded with a steady stream of customers. Many old faces were back, along with new ones, as Ariana found out when she went to the dry goods aisle to organize ten-pound bags of rice. She came upon two women she'd never seen before.

"So did you hear?" whispered a portly woman, poking a bag of green lentils. "There's a feud between this store and the one that opened across the plaza."

"Oh, yes," said the other woman in a pink *chador*. "My sister heard about it at Ali's Auto Repair Shop when she took her car in for an oil change. I'm going to check out their prices after getting the free bread here."

Ariana slunk away to restock the pickles. Obviously gossip about the stores had spread to neighboring towns. *Whatever,* she thought, thinking back to the picture of the European green crab. It was survival of the fittest, and it didn't matter what kind of customers they were getting, as long as they were the paying kind.

With the recent uptick in customers, the kids had been put on a rotating schedule to help at the store. Friday afternoon it was Ariana's and Laila's turn, and it was particularly busy, since everyone was picking up groceries for the weekend. Ariana had just reorganized the new freezer, packed with a new line of chicken and lamb kebobs when she noticed a gap in the coffee section. She ran back to the storage room, passing Uncle Shams, who was on the phone happily reordering supplies.

As she sorted through cardboard boxes, muffled shouts filtered over from the bakery. Ariana grimaced, feeling sorry for the new assistant baker her father had hired to help Haroon. She grabbed a dozen cartons of tea and exited, pausing a moment at the bakery door.

Haroon stood with his hands on his hips, glaring

at a row of singed, smoking bread. "What were you thinking?" he barked.

Sweat ran down the assistant's thin face, and his elbows were covered in flour. "Apologies, Haroon sahib," he mumbled, wiping his forehead with a towel. "I'm just figuring out how the ovens work. The one in the corner is rather tricky."

"I told you how to do it five times!" growled Haroon. "An idiot from the village could do it—and we were already behind to begin with!"

"A thousand apologies . . . ," said the assistant, hurrying to lug in a bag of flour.

"This free bread is killing me," grumbled Haroon, throwing up his hands.

Ariana scooted off, leaving the men to start another batch of dough. Since the free bread campaign had started two weeks before, Haroon had been baking three times as much bread, and Ariana wasn't a bit surprised that he was grumpier than usual.

By late afternoon most customers had gone home, so Ariana and Laila grabbed bottles of orange soda and took a break before Nasreen came to pick them up. An exhausted feeling of satisfaction settled over Ariana as she took a gulp of ice-cold soda. This was a *good* tired. They were winning against stinking Pamir Market.

She glanced at her father, proud that he'd come up with the free bread campaign, and spotted Uncle Shams stepping outside for a breath of fresh air. Suddenly her uncle stiffened, and Ariana followed his gaze across the plaza. He was glaring at Gulbadin Ghilzai, who'd just stepped out of his car, a sleek red BMW. The two men eyed each other a moment, but Gulbadin turned in a huff and marched off toward his store. Uncle Shams pivoted and headed over to chat with Mr. Milan.

Back inside, Jamil balanced the accounting ledger while the television buzzed in the background. Ariana found Laila's eyes glued to the newscaster's fire-engine-red lips.

"Scenes of carnage today in the Paktia Province, on the border of Afghanistan and Pakistan," said the woman, showing a clip of a bombed-out village. "Villagers report of an attack that occurred before dawn . . ."

Ariana sighed, not wanting to hear about battles, guns, and destruction, so she tuned out the news and edged toward the window.

The plaza was nearly empty as the sun set in the distance, and the hot-pink neon sign for Wong Plaza flickered to life. The G in "Wong" remained dark, announcing Won Plaza. In the fuchsia light Ariana noticed that the entire sign looked pretty beat up. Mr. Martinez stood chatting with his delivery guy over crates of avocados and bell peppers. She and Laila still hadn't made it over to Juan More Tacos to get the chips and salsa he'd offered all those weeks before. She ran her gaze past Milan's Indian Emporium to Well-Read Secondhand Books and mentally kicked herself as she glanced at the cracked window. The sale sign was long gone, and she'd forgotten to get origami paper. Her supply was running low.

With a sigh she glanced at Koo Koo Dry Cleaning's awning, bleached by the sun and saggy in the middle, to Hooper's Diner, with its FOR LEASE sign. It had closed nearly a year before, after Mr. Hooper's heart attack. Neither of his sons had wanted to take over the business, so Mrs. Wong was desperately looking for a new tenant. As if noticing the plaza for the first time, Ariana realized that all the stores looked a bit shabby and outdated. Besides Pamir Market, which had been renovated before opening, the rest of the buildings needed a fresh coat of paint and a face-lift, Kabul Corner included.

Mariam was at the house when they arrived, and Ariana was thrilled. She hadn't had the chance to hang out with her in weeks, and she was dying to show Mariam the new origami animals.

But Mariam's words stopped her cold. "Hey, guys. I'm so glad you're back. Laila and I have a lot of work to do. Noor got me a bunch of beetles."

"Where did your sister get these?" asked Laila, looking nervously into the box.

"From a pet store near her university," said Mariam.

Ariana stood, stony-faced, as Laila gave Mariam an excited grin.

"Don't worry," Mariam told Laila. "The beetles are already dead. Noor said they use them to feed the frogs or something gross like that. It's going to be *so* cool to mummify them."

"Oh," said Ariana. "I guess you won't need me, then, so I'll be in my room." *My stinky, crowded room that's not really mine.*

"No, silly," said Mariam. "I haven't seen you in, like, forever. Sit with us, please. I want us to hang out while we work."

"Okay," said Ariana, feeling a bit better.

As Laila disappeared into the hall to get her books, Mariam grabbed Ariana's arm, pausing to check for nosey ears, and whispered, "We have to talk."

Ariana tensed. "Okay," she mumbled. "Let me get some juice first."

As she grabbed two apple juice cartons from the pantry, she dawdled, thinking back to the day she'd first met Mariam, nearly six years before. Her parents had invited Mariam's family over for dinner, since their fathers had recently become friends. At first Ariana hadn't even noticed the silent, skinny little girl shadowing her older brother, Fadi. From the grown-ups' whispers Ariana had learned that Mariam had accidently been left behind in Afghanistan when her family had fled to escape the Taliban. Somehow the gutsy little girl had ended up in a refugee camp in Pakistan and had eventually been reunited with her family. It had been Fadi who'd found Mariam in a photograph of a refugee camp, clinging to Gulmina, her Barbie doll wearing a bright pink burka.

Amazed by her story, Ariana had tentatively approached Mariam, sensing that behind the fear lurked a spunky girl who needed time to come out of her shell. At first Mariam had resisted, but when Ariana had showed her a bag of chocolate-dipped Oreos, Mariam had given her a shy smile. The two girls had spent the rest of the evening watching *A*

Charlie Brown Christmas, with Mariam glued to the screen, Gulmina by her side. Ariana had later found out that after arriving in America, Mariam had suffered from an anxiety disorder because of her horrific experience of being left behind in Afghanistan, and the only thing that had calmed her down had been watching television. So for the first few months, her parents had let her watch endless hours of black-and-white movies, cartoons, game shows, and old sitcoms. As she'd reverted back to her old self, Mariam had picked up a dramatic flair and a love for the performing arts. Ariana and Mariam had been inseparable since that day and had even begun first grade together, because even though Mariam was a year older, she had missed a year of school. When Mariam said, "We have to talk," it was something serious.

Maybe she doesn't want to be friends anymore. Maybe she likes Laila better. Who wouldn't? Laila was fun, pretty, and perfect. I'm grumpy, uninteresting, and totally awkward. Her stomach sank to her ankles as she walked back into the dining room.

"I was in the bathroom stall the other day, and I overheard Patty, Yoojin, and their posse talking," said Mariam, her hazel eyes stern.

"Huh?" mumbled Ariana. *This isn't about us?*

"You won't believe what they were saying," said Mariam, leaning forward.

"What?" The fear of losing Mariam's friendship morphed into an unknown anxiety.

"They said you were a *bully*—and *mean*—that you had something against Wali, who they think is really nice and supercute, by the way."

"Oh, crud," said Ariana. It wasn't like she was ever going to be best friends with Patty and her crew, but she didn't want to be on their bad side either.

"I walked out of the stall, gave them a dirty look, and stomped out!"

Ariana grinned, imagining the scene in her head.

"So they know that I know what they are saying. So if rumors start, they know that I know—that you know—it's them."

"You're awesome." Ariana grinned.

"Yeah! It was hilarious, but then I found this," she said, passing Ariana a copy of the school newspaper. The third article in *The Owl* was about bullying. Mariam had underlined a section that talked about "certain aggressive individuals in school who pick on people."

"Oh, no," muttered Ariana.

"Patty is the editor of the newspaper," said Mariam,

"so she probably means *you*. We need to work on damage control. . . ." Ten minutes later, as they finished up talking about how to repair Ariana's reputation, Laila still hadn't returned.

Ariana changed the subject, happy to have her best friend to herself. "I still can't believe you applied for us to be on the *Great Race* together," she said, grinning at the memory.

"Hey, we would have been an amazing team and kicked some serious butt," exclaimed Mariam, still upset with the producers of the show. She and Ariana had actually made it to their short list, but when they'd called Mariam's house and found out she was twelve and Ariana was eleven, not even the minimum age of eighteen, the girls had been disqualified.

"It sure would have been fun racing around the world on a scavenger hunt," agreed Ariana. "I caught the episode the week before last, and the remaining four teams were in China, looking for clues along the Great Wall."

"Man . . . we so could have won a hundred thousand dollars," said Mariam. "I'm so mad, I'm not watching the show this year in protest."

"Oh," said Ariana. She hadn't realized the depth of Mariam's anger toward the producers, so she changed the subject. "Can you believe that Rodrigo got tossed off *Supreme Chef*?"

"I know," Mariam said with a sigh. "They dinged him just because his soufflé didn't rise properly. I was so bummed to see him go—and that mean chef from New York, Hilary, is still there, hiding ingredients from people so that they'll lose," continued Mariam. "Hey, that reminds me, my parents are letting me watch another really cool reality show."

"Which one?" asked Ariana. She knew Mariam's parents didn't approve of her lingering fascination with television and carefully monitored what she watched.

"It's called *Take That*," said Mariam.

"Take *what*?" asked Ariana, a little confused.

"No, Ari. *Take That*," repeated Mariam. "It's a show where victims who've been bamboozled confront the people who've scammed them."

"That doesn't sound that interesting," said Ariana.

"No, you totally *have* to watch it," said Mariam, her eyes earnest. "In the last episode a guy named José confronted his mechanic, Archie, when he found out that his brand-new engine had been replaced with an old, beat up one. José ended up finding out that the Archie had been cheating people for years. In the end José got his money back and helped shut down Archie's mechanic shop. The show's all about getting power back from people who swindle you."

"Oh," said Ariana, still not fully convinced she'd watch, though the premise of the show was intriguing.

"Where is she?" wondered Mariam five minutes later. It was pretty late, and Ariana's mother would be calling them to dinner soon.

Ariana shrugged, not particularly caring. This was like old times; just her and Mariam, arguing over who the best contestant was on *America's Next Big Voice*.

"Laila," Mariam called out. "Come on. We need to get started."

There was no response, and no Laila.

7

Runaway Baker

"WHAT HAPPENED TO HER?" asked Mariam.

"Who knows," grumbled Ariana.

"We need to go look," said Mariam, getting up from her chair.

Reluctantly Ariana rose. Laila wasn't on the first level of the house, so they headed upstairs. It was unusually quiet since the younger boys were next door getting help with long division from Sara *Khala*. Finally they found Laila in the master bedroom, along with Zainab *Khala*, Ariana's mother, and Hava Bibi. Zainab *Khala*'s face was streaked with tears, and Laila's eyes were suspiciously wet.

"What's wrong?" asked Ariana.

"We just got a call from Afghanistan, *jaan*," said Nasreen. "Laila's father was . . . injured, but *alhamdu-lillah*, not seriously."

Laila hid her face in a tissue as Mariam went over to sit beside her. Ariana stood rooted to her spot, uncertain what to do.

"Don't worry, *jaan*. Your father will be okay," said Hava Bibi. "He's safe at the military hospital and will be up and running in no time."

"You grandmother is right," said Nasreen, adjusting her silk blouse that tucked into a slim skirt. "You girls have a lot of schoolwork to do. We will call the hospital tonight, and Laila, you can talk to your father then."

Slowly Laila got up, assisted by Mariam, and all three girls returned to the dining room.

"What happened?" Ariana blurted out.

"It was an IED, on the road to Gardez," said Laila. Her shoulders slumped as she sat down.

Ariana shuddered. She knew what an IED, an improvised explosive device, was capable of. It was a homemade bomb that not only killed but horribly maimed people.

"Oh, no," whispered Mariam, patting Laila on the back.

Laila sat in her chair, staring straight ahead, as if she couldn't quite digest the news. "Gardez is an ancient city located between two important roads that cut through a huge valley," she rambled, clutching her locket. "It has always been an important spot for plundering armies; even Alexander the Great had posts there when he tried to invade in 330 B.C."

"Uh, sure," said Mariam, sharing a confused look with Ariana.

Ariana shrugged, not quite knowing how to comfort her cousin either.

"Gardez is very close to Tora Bora," said Laila, blinking slowly, as if in a daze. "That's where Osama bin Laden and Mullah Omar, the leader of the Taliban, escaped to when the Americans went looking for them after 9/11."

"Oh," said Ariana. She remembered only fragments from 9/11, since she'd been too young to fully understand the terrible day, six years ago. That's when Bin Laden had attacked America by sending planes crashing into the Twin Towers in New York City and into the Pentagon in Washington, DC. Bin Laden, once a wealthy businessman, had initially come to Afghanistan to help the people fight the Soviets. He'd been a respected figure, even by the American government, which had supplied him with weapons to fight the Soviets.

"My father and his unit of American soldiers had gone to Gardez with a group of Polish soldiers," continued Laila, "to investigate a sighting of Taliban forces."

Ariana's stomach clenched. She remembered hearing bits of this story on the news. The realization that it involved her family made it feel very real. She imagined her father being shot, and her hands went cold.

"One of the Polish soldiers was killed—the first Polish casualty since Poland joined the war in Afghanistan," said Laila, tears glistening in her green eyes.

Mariam sucked in her breath, going pale.

"Mariam, you okay?" said Ariana. One crying person was hard to handle. Two would be *way* too much.

"Yeah, I'm okay," said Mariam, squeezing Laila's hand. "Like Nasreen *Khala* said, your dad will be back on his feet in no time."

"I want to go home," Laila said in a strangled whisper.

Ariana leaned forward in surprise. "You want to go back to Afghanistan? But it's so dangerous—you couldn't even go to school."

"Our house is there," whispered Laila. "I miss my

room; our garden; my best friend, Saima; and the ice cream vendor who always saved me my favorite flavor—mango."

Ariana was speechless. *Laila didn't want to leave Afghanistan.* She'd assumed that her cousin had wanted to move to America, since Uncle Hamza had such a dangerous job that put his life in danger. Translators like him, and their families, were allowed to immigrate to the United States, so that's how Laila and her mother had come. Uncle Hamza was supposed to follow in December. As Ariana remembered the times she'd wished that her cousins hadn't come, an uncomfortable sensation of guilt lodged near her heart.

Laila fumbled to open the gold filigreed pendant that hung from her neck, and held it out. Tucked on one side was a tiny picture of Laila and her father, sitting in the garden of their old house in Kabul. The other side held a picture of a boy, a little younger than Zayd, a mischievous smile on his lips, and deep, sea-green eyes.

"Who's that?" asked Mariam, pointing to the boy.

"Lawang," whispered Laila. "He was my brother."

"Was?" said Ariana, her eyes wide.

"He died two years ago," said Laila, blinking back a fresh round of tears.

"How?" Mariam gasped.

"He came back from school one day with a fever. But it kept getting worse," explained Laila. "He lost his appetite and had severe headaches, so my father took him to the hospital. Within a week he was gone."

Ariana gripped the side of the table as she remembered a conversation between Hava Bibi and her mother last year. They had been speaking mainly in Pukhto, and Ariana had strained to hear the hushed, worried conversation. All she'd picked up was that someone's son had died in Kabul. At the time she'd felt sympathy for the boy's death, but since she didn't know who it was, she had soon forgotten about it.

"What was wrong with him?" asked Mariam.

"They never found out," said Laila, her face stiff.

"Why not?" whispered Ariana, her throat tight, not understanding how one minute you could have a fever and then the next minute be dead.

Laila looked at Ariana with eyes that seemed far older than her thirteen years. "That's how it is in Afghanistan, Ariana *jaan*. The hospitals are not equipped to deal with serious illness. People die all the time, especially kids."

As Ariana stared at Lawang's portrait, she remembered Laila hugging and kissing Omar and Hasan.

They probably reminded her of Lawang. It dawned on Ariana that she'd been so lost in the resentment of having a perfect cousin invade her life that she knew practically nothing about Laila.

Suddenly Laila reached over and grabbed Ariana's arm, staring at her intently. "I'm so sorry, Ariana, but I was so jealous of you," she whispered.

"What?" mumbled Ariana, further taken aback.

Laila twisted her *kameez* in her hands and shifted her gaze. "When I arrived, all I could think of was how lucky you were," she whispered. "You had a wonderful home, a loving family, and a best friend who would do anything for you."

Ariana sat, speechless, as shame settled over her like a thick layer of jam—sticky and uncomfortable. Ariana had been so busy envying the attention Laila was getting that she hadn't once thought about how Laila felt.

"And you're so confident and smart," added Laila.

Ariana reached out and took Laila's hand. "No, please—you don't understand. Please don't feel bad. Actually, I was jealous of you, too."

"What?" said Laila, her head bobbing up.

"You're the smart one," said Ariana. "You fit into the family better than I ever have. You speak Pukhto and Farsi beautifully and are so helpful around the house and the store. Everyone loves you."

The two girls sat looking at each other with growing embarrassment.

Mariam laughed with delight, giving them both a hug. "Look at you two buttheads! You're both awesome in your own ways."

As Ariana looked at Laila and Mariam together, the long festering knot in her chest began to ease.

"You'll make friends here," said Mariam, turning to Laila. "When I came, I met Ariana, and we've been best friends ever since."

"Uncle Hamza will be here at the end of December," added Ariana. "You'll be together again and find a place to call home."

Laila sat mute, looking unconvinced.

"I loved our old house in Kabul too," said Mariam. "My dad was a professor at the university, but the Taliban came into power, and it became too dangerous for us to stay. As we were leaving, when I was six, I got lost in the rush of people trying to climb onto the truck headed to the Pakistan border."

Laila gasped. "What?"

"Well, it all turned out okay." Mariam smiled. "I was found."

"But how were you left?" pushed Laila, news about her father forgotten.

"It wasn't anyone's fault, really. My brother, Fadi, was holding my hand, and I let it go to pick up my Gulmina, my Barbie."

"So it was his fault," said Laila.

"No, it wasn't his fault," said Mariam. "He was just a kid like us, but he blamed himself for a long time—"

Suddenly the front door burst open. It was Uncle Shams, and he was breathing heavily. "Jamil. Brother, come quick!" he shouted.

The girls quieted as Jamil emerged from the garage. "What's going on?"

"It's a catastrophe, a true calamity, I tell you," Shams said, and wept.

"What happened? What is such a calamity?" asked Jamil, confronting his brother.

"That ungrateful wretch, that toad, I can't believe what he did!"

"Shams, who are you talking about? What happened?"

"Haroon, that piece of donkey dung!"

"What about him?"

"He quit!"

"What?" Jamil gasped. "What do you mean, he quit?"

"And he wasn't man enough to tell me himself. He sent me a text. Can you believe it? A text!"

"But what happened? Where did he go?"

Uncle Shams pulled out his phone and scrolled through his messages. "The ornery fool said he was overworked, underpaid, and unappreciated. So he's gone."

"He's quit before," said Jamil, trying to calm his brother down. "Remember three years ago? He wanted new ovens and a raise. We gave it to him. So ask him what he wants, and he'll be back."

Two hours later, as the girls sat in the dining room pretending to do their homework, the truth of what had happened to Haroon became apparent. Uncle Shams called around and figured out what had happened, sharing the news with Jamil, Nasreen, and his wife as they huddled together in the living room. Haroon, it turned out, had been lured away to bake his famous bread for someone else—and that someone was Pamir Market.

8

Mystery Meat

AT FIRST ARIANA DIDN'T notice the vivid fragments of sunburst yellow plastered throughout Wong Plaza. She had eyes only for the sign that had been hanging in Pamir Market's front window: BAKERY NOW OPEN. SERVING FRESH, DELICIOUS BREAD. Her ears filled with a dull roar, her vision blurring. The Ghilzais had stolen the Shinwaris' prized baker right out from under their noses, and now Haroon was in *there,* baking the same incredible loaves that had attracted Kabul Corner's customers—customers that had now been reduced to a trickle.

The evening Haroon had disappeared, Nasreen

had suggested that the brothers go after him and offer more money, a car, new ovens, and an assistant— anything to get him back, but the cantankerous baker had avoided their efforts to contact him. Ariana had sat nearby, wondering if she could have foreseen what had happened and stopped it somehow. She'd seen Haroon at the bakery earlier that day, more frustrated and angry than usual. Maybe she should have told her father. But now was too late. The baker was already gone. Hava Bibi had bustled in then, trying to be the voice of reason, reminding her sons that Haroon had left before and that they shouldn't blame the Ghilzais without proof. But Jamil, usually the even-tempered one, had become gruff, regretting his friendliness to Gulbadin.

While sweeping the sidewalk, Mrs. Milan waved as Jamil parked the car in front of Kabul Corner. Ariana and Zayd waved back, watching their neighbors ready their stores for a slow Sunday morning.

Their father paused at the door, keys in hand. "What is this?" he murmured, ripping a bright yellow flyer off the front door.

Zayd leaned over his father's shoulder and read out loud. "*Friends and neighbors, BEWARE! It has come to our attention that the new store in Wong Plaza, Pamir*

Market, is involved in nefarious activities. Their so-called 100 percent halal beef is actually horse meat!"

"What is this nonsense?" said Jamil with a frown.

"Huh?" squeaked Ariana. "Can horse meat be halal?"

"Well, actually, it can," said Zayd, dredging up an old Sunday school lecture. "To be considered halal, meat must come from animals that are herbivores and have hooves. Plus they need to be slaughtered in a humane way while taking God's name, so that the killing of an innocent animal is accepted. The Jews have a similar process, except it's called 'kosher.'"

"That's *way* too much information," said Ariana with a shudder, not wanting to *really* think about where her hamburger came from.

"Get this," said Zayd, warming up to the topic in the way only a true nerd could. He flipped through the Internet on his phone, and Jamil continued reading the flyer, his frown deepening. "Horse meat is pretty popular in other countries. They make sausage out of it in Austria, called *leberkäse*; a stew, *pastissada*, in Italy; and cold cuts in Sweden!"

"Gross. Stop it already," yelped Ariana, beginning to feel a little queasy. She pushed past Zayd and leaned over to read the flyer herself.

The notice continued to tell concerned citizens to

avoid shopping at Pamir Market, as they could not be trusted. The top half of the flyer was in English, and the bottom was in Farsi script, which Ariana couldn't read that well.

"Wow. Someone really went to town when putting these all over the place," called out Mr. Martinez from across the street, waving a flyer as Jamil shrugged in confusion.

"Dad, who put these up?" asked Zayd as they all walked into the store.

"I have no idea, *bachay*," said Jamil. "I need to call your uncle."

Zayd and Ariana exchanged a worried look and got out the brooms to start the usual routine. The store wouldn't open for another half hour. Ariana had just made sure the scoops were in all the nut bins when she heard furious pounding on the front door. She turned to see her father flip open the lock.

Gulbadin Ghilzai stood at the door, his face a mottled shade of red beneath a dense brown beard. Wali was behind him, lips compressed in a tight line. Gulbadin waved a crumpled flyer in his pudgy fist. "How dare you print such lies?"

Jamil raised his hands in confusion. "We had nothing to do with them."

"You came to me and *pretended* to welcome us to the plaza, and now you do this?" barked Gulbadin, his round frame shivering like a bowl of Jell-O.

"I didn't pretend, and we did not put those up," said Jamil in an even tone, though his sense of *nang* had been insulted.

"Of course you did! Don't lie to me," shrilled Gulbadin. "Who else would benefit from such outrageous slander?"

"Maybe you did it," said Jamil, narrowing his eyes. "Maybe you put these up so you could blame us for harassing you. After all, you did steal our baker. It seems you will stoop to anything to succeed."

"How dare you suggest I stole Haroon! He came to us. Obviously he wasn't happy at your second-rate store."

Jamil stiffened. "We were here first, before you came along with your underhanded price-cutting."

"Underhanded? That's called smart business. But instead of playing fair, it seems that the only way you can drum up customers is to lie about the competition!"

"On my honor, I tell you, we did not have anything to do with the flyers," growled Jamil.

Ariana looked out the window and saw Mr.

Martinez come out of his restaurant to whisper with Mrs. Smith. The Milans had also wandered outside to see what the ruckus was about. Ariana glanced at Wali and froze when his heated gaze fell on her. She clenched the broom in her hand and jerked her eyes away.

Gulbadin threw the flyer on the ground and spat on it. "That is what I think of your honor," he said, shaking his finger at Jamil. "This is defamation. I will have Lucinda throw you out. . . . I . . . I will sue you!"

"Go ahead, you fool!" shouted Jamil, and he slammed the door in Gulbadin's face. Then he stood there, shocked at his own behavior.

Ariana stood trembling, and exchanged a horrified look with Zayd.

"Oh, man," whispered Zayd.

They'd never seen their father lose his temper like that before. Ariana reached over to grab Zayd's hand as he stared out the window. They saw the crowd of onlookers watching Gulbadin and Wali storming back to Pamir Market, ripping off flyers as they went.

"It'll be okay," whispered Zayd. "Dad will figure out what the heck is going on." Ariana nodded, and they returned to work.

Fifteen minutes later Uncle Shams arrived, his sky-blue minivan screeching to a halt in front of the store. Just as Jamil finished explaining what had happened, Lucinda Wong arrived, her iron-gray hair windblown, lines of worry marring her forehead. Like two naughty schoolboys, Jamil and Shams stood beside the register while Lucinda waved her finger at them, holding a copy of the flyer.

"Jamil, Shams, what is going on? I just got a call from Gulbadin, and he was so angry, he could barely get a word out. He's threatening to sue everyone!"

"We don't know where the flyers came from," said Shams.

"They were here before we arrived this morning," added Jamil.

"These are very serious accusations Gulbadin is leveling against you," said Lucinda, wringing her hands. "I don't know what to make of it. I know you were very upset when I gave Gulbadin a lease to open a similar store—"

"We were unhappy, but we would never do anything like this," interjected Jamil.

"Well, it looks bad," said Lucinda, pacing the checkered linoleum floor. "If you look at the facts, you're the only ones who'd benefit from the allegations on the flyer."

"But we didn't do this," said Shams, bristling at the accusation. Jamil squeezed his arm, trying to calm him down.

Lucinda sighed and gave them a sad look. "I've known you boys for more than a decade, and you've been excellent tenants. You've never caused any problems, and always paid me on time."

"We swear on our honor," said Jamil. "We had nothing to do with these flyers, regardless of how upset we were about the new store."

"I should have installed security cameras years ago," grumbled Lucinda, throwing up her hands. "That way we would have video footage of who posted the flyers. But during these lean financial times, I can't afford to."

Or afford a new coat of paint and other fixes around the plaza either, thought Ariana, hidden behind the spice rack.

"Since there is no proof of who did this, I will let you go with a warning," said Lucinda, "but I don't want any more trouble."

Ariana stopped scrubbing her hair in the soothing warm water when she heard someone enter her parents' bedroom. She'd snuck into the master bathroom to soak in the tub, since the twins were hogging the one in the hallway.

"We may have to forfeit our deposit on the new house, Nasreen *jaan*," came her father's subdued voice.

Ariana froze, sensing that the word "forfeit" meant trouble.

"What do you mean, Jamil?" responded Nasreen, her voice confused.

Her father sighed and paused for a moment. "With all the trouble at the store, we don't have a steady source of income to pay for a mortgage. We have to face the reality that Haroon is gone for good and all those customers who came to get their bread from us now go to Pamir Market."

"But the situation is temporary, right?" asked Nasreen. "Business should pick up once you find another baker."

"Shams and I have been looking," said Jamil. "But we can't find a replacement who's as good, or reliable. So far this has been the worst month of business we've had since we opened. We barely covered the cost of running the store—the electricity, water, and inventory."

"Oh my goodness," said Nasreen, her voice weak.

Ariana slumped against the smooth porcelain,

her dream of her own room popping like a watermelon-scented bubble.

"It's okay, Jamil," said Nasreen. "Of course I'm disappointed, and the kids will be too, especially Ariana. But if this is what Allah wills, then so be it. *Insha'*Allah things will turn around at the store."

"I hope so too," said Jamil. "We won't make a decision yet. Let's just see how things go."

Shock settled over Ariana's skin like a layer of numbing ice. *I really need to stop listening to other people's conversations,* she thought. *All I hear is bad news.* She heard the floor creak, and hoped neither of her parents tried to open the bathroom door. But heck, it wasn't as if she'd been eavesdropping on purpose. *I'm only trying to take a bath, for heaven's sake!* But she didn't have to worry, since her parents left. Deflated by the news, she slowly dried off, slipped on her soft seamless flannel pajamas, and headed downstairs.

On her way through the foyer, she spotted a vivid splash of yellow. It was the flyer her father had taken from the store door. She grabbed it from the hall table with shaking fingers and slunk into the garage. The calendar with its bright red *X*s hung in the corner as Charlie Brown and Snoopy held hands while doing a happy dance. The glee on their little cartoon faces sent a burst of anger through her heart. *How can they be so happy when I'm miserable?* Overcome with a mixture of anger and grief, she wanted to rip it from the wall, but she clenched her fist, holding back the urge. *I'm not going to give up hope.* She grabbed the red marker and drew a bold red *X* on today's date. She also drew a big mustache across Charlie Brown's upper lip, then turned her back on him.

Feeling a bit better, she flipped on the table lamp and sat down, smoothing out the bright yellow flyer on the desk. She wanted to think of something, anything, that didn't remind her of the awful news her parents had inadvertently shared with her. She stared down at the ugly message on the page. Ironically, the paper the message was written on was beautiful—heavyweight, in a rich shade of sunflower yellow, one of Ariana's favorites. She would have loved to get a paint swatch to match it for her new room . . . a room she probably wasn't going to get now. Tears welled up in her eyes, and then she got angry at herself. *I'm not going to let stupid Wali and his family make me cry.*

She dried her tears and smoothed out the paper's textured surface. She pulled out her magnifying glass and saw that it was well made, which was odd. Usually mass-produced flyers used cheap copy paper, like her father's flyers, some of which were still stacked on the desk. She tore part of the yellow flyer and saw that it frayed ever so slightly, which meant that it was made of more expensive cotton pulp. This was no cheap stock paper. It was sturdy, great for origami. As she ran her finger along the surface, the tip of her finger became stained with a hint of ink. She rubbed her father's flyer, and its ink stayed true. *Who would go to so much trouble to use good quality paper for a mass-produced flyer? The ink is different too. What a waste of money.*

She knew that her father and uncle hadn't had anything to do with the mystery meat flyers. *But could it really be the Ghilzais?* Gulbadin could have had these printed up to accuse the Shinwaris of harassment, but that just didn't make any sense, especially since an accusation like this could damage Pamir Market's reputation. If customers really believed that the Ghilzais were selling horse meat as beef, everyone would be grossed out and wouldn't step foot into their store. She reread the section in English and found no clues as to who could be behind the flyer. She traced her fingers along the curved Farsi script, but despite all her mother's efforts to teach her, she couldn't read it. Maybe Hava Bibi could translate it for her. But no, her grandmother was at Uncle Shams's town house next door. That left her parents, whom she didn't want to bother. So that left one other person in the house who could read it.

A frown marred Laila's usually smooth brow as she contemplated the Farsi script. Ariana sat next to her, tapping her foot impatiently as her cousin carefully reread the words over and over again, checking her Farsi-to-English dictionary.

"This is really badly written," said Laila, turning to Ariana. "It's a literal translation—as if someone took an English-to-Farsi dictionary and just transcribed it, word by word, from English to Farsi. The grammar is really poor, and it sounds funny."

"So whoever wrote it doesn't know Farsi that well?" Ariana pondered as Laila nodded. "But Gulbadin and his family are fluent in Farsi," said Ariana.

Laila nodded, confusion marring her features. "I don't know why they would create such a badly written flyer, especially since it would hurt their business."

Ariana frowned. It made no sense. *No sense at all.* "There's something fishy going on here."

"Fishy?" repeated Laila.

Ariana laughed. "It's an Americanism. It means that something suspicious is going on—something doesn't smell right."

"Oh. This is definitely fishy," said Laila, looking at the flyer, her bright aquamarine eyes serious.

"Thank you, Laila," said Ariana, "for helping me with this."

"Why would you thank me?" said Laila, frowning. "We are family—we help each other, no matter what."

Ariana gazed into Laila's face and found sincerity, along with a quizzical smile. It seemed like the envy and bitter feelings they'd held against each other were now a slowly fading memory. She returned Laila's smile, though her heart felt heavy. Something about the flyer just didn't feel right.

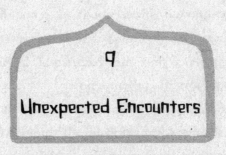

9

Unexpected Encounters

EIGHT SLEEPY KIDS, ALONG with Uncle Shams, squeezed into the minivan and headed toward Lake Elizabeth Park for the annual Festival of the Arts. Ariana sat in the third row, pressed against the window; she'd made sure not to get stuck in the middle of the boys. Laila was at the other end, watching Marjan drool in his sleep. She and Ariana shared a grin and settled in for the ride. Ariana sleepily rested her face against the cold glass, watching the sun inch up from beyond the hills. She spotted her mother and Sara *Khala*'s crimson polka dot dress in the rearview mirror, following behind in the truck, which was packed with supplies. Her father was at the store, since it was open for business on Sunday. After the appearance of the flyers accusing Pamir Market of selling horse meat, business at Kabul Corner had picked up. But she didn't know if it was enough . . . enough for the new house. And she didn't dare bring up the topic with her parents, since they hadn't told the kids anything about forfeiting their deposit.

For the past six years Kabul Corner had had a booth at the festival—a mini stop for all things Afghan—pickles, jams, cookies, and a line of Afghan handcrafts made by women widowed during the country's many wars. Nasreen and Sara *Khala* had started a nonprofit business to help these women by selling their beautiful beaded handbags, embroidered shoes, and silver jewelry in America, then sending the money back to them.

Uncle Shams was lucky enough to find a parking spot close to the same booth they reserved every year, and Nasreen and Sara *Khala* pulled into the spot next to them. The kids tumbled out of the minivan, like sardines exiting a tin can.

"Ah, here we are again," said Uncle Shams, taking a swig from his thermos of sweet tea.

Yes, indeed, thought Ariana grumpily, peering down

the street, which was shut down, allowing vendors to prepare their stalls. *Here we are again.* She eyed the line of booths, numbering close to seven hundred, wishing she were back in bed, snuggled beneath her soft quilt, listening to a snoring Hava Bibi.

"Okay, guys," said Uncle Shams, rubbing his hands against the morning chill. "Get the tables out of the truck and start unloading."

Zayd opened the truck doors, and the twins, wearing matching red woolen caps, climbed inside. Jointly carrying a foldable table, Ariana and Laila trekked over to booth 412, near one of the three entertainment stages, conveniently across from the food pavilion. The heavenly scent of frying funnel cakes, hot dogs, and cotton candy had begun to waft through the air. Ariana's stomach rumbled. Her brothers had finished the last of the cereal that morning, and there was no way she was going to touch a fried egg. A hot dog slathered with mustard sure sounded good right now. In addition to the usual fair food, many local restaurants and food trucks served their specialties—Thai noodles, falafel pitas, spicy tandoori chicken, and tacos brimming with shredded beef.

"No dawdling!" barked Uncle Shams as Baz and Marjan hauled boxes. "Okay, my beloved," he said to his wife. "I need to talk to my buddies on the organization committee."

"All right, *jaan*," said Sara *Khala*, spreading out the red tablecloths.

"Call me if you need me," said Uncle Shams, and he disappeared into the crowd.

Even though sales had picked up after the appearance of the mystery meat flyers, Ariana knew that her father and uncle were still brainstorming about how to bring in more customers. So Uncle Shams's goal at the festival was to do as much marketing as possible to drum up business. *We're fighting extinction*, she thought glumly. *It's the survival of the fittest.* In quiet companionship, she and Laila unpacked boxes, arranged packets of nuts, and stacked jars of honey in neat pyramids while watching the blues band onstage tune their instruments. Nasreen handed Ariana the wax earplugs she usually wore so that the music didn't bother her too much during the long day. The festival officially opened at ten, and they had just a couple of hours to set up.

Ariana laid out the hand-stitched purses, her mind wandering back to the flyers about Pamir Market. She and Laila had talked about it a lot over the past few days, and the more they discussed it, the more certain they felt that the Ghilzais couldn't possibly be behind them; it just didn't make sense to try to discredit their own store. *But if it wasn't them, who was it?* she thought, perplexed. They'd wanted to talk to Ariana's father about it, but whenever they'd seen him, his lips had been tight with worry about shrinking revenues, and they'd kept silent. They had no proof that the Ghilzais *hadn't* distributed the flyers, and they didn't have an alternative culprit who could be responsible. With a deep sigh Ariana tugged open another box of scarves, preparing for a long day ahead.

"I'm so tired, I could pass out," whined Omar as Baz collapsed on the grass, earning a dark look from Zayd.

Ariana agreed and passed her water bottle over to Hasan, who gave her a grateful smile. They'd been standing at the booth for hours, and she was tired of smiling and trying to explain the knot count on the half dozen handwoven carpets they had on display. Basically, the greater the number of knots that made up a rug, the better the quality. You had to flip a corner of the rug over to show interested customers the intricate rows of knots. Most people thought it was amazing that a girl her age knew this, but hey, she was Afghan. Most Afghans had dozens of carpets in their house, and kids grew up knowing good quality from bad, especially her, since her sensitive fingers could detect the quality of wool from its texture within seconds.

Somewhere in the next row Ariana could hear Uncle Shams talking to the other vendors, picking up news, talking about Kabul Corner's new line of frozen foods. His voice grew louder as he came closer, and Ariana saw that he was with an elegant older woman dressed in a neat black suit and turquoise blouse. She stood out from the casually attired crowd, especially since she was trailed by a group of equally well-dressed assistants, shaking hands, passing out leaflets.

"This is our booth," said Uncle Shams, smiling widely. He introduced her to Nasreen and Sara *Khala*. "This is Ana Cardoso. She's a retired pediatrician from the school education board. She's running for mayor."

"Of course," said Nasreen, grabbing a leaflet and sticking it into the money box. "We've been following the race very closely.

Really? thought Ariana. She'd never seen her mother pay attention to local politics, though Nasreen voted during presidential elections and watched international news closely. *Maybe this is what adults call white lies.*

"It's a very close race, so we need your vote," said Ana, shaking their hands.

"We're very concerned about the funding cuts at the school," said Sara *Khala*, who was forever complaining about the standards dropping.

Ariana nodded. Because of California's state budget cuts, school funding had been sharply reduced. At Brookhaven they'd nearly lost their art class, while physical education and band had been reduced to twice a week. Not that she played any instruments, but Mariam did—the trombone.

"We're all concerned, and education is my number one priority," said Ana with a sad shake of her head.

"Good," said Sara *Khala* and Nasreen together.

"As a mother of two girls, I know the importance of education and the access to quality health care," said Ana. "The Fremont police and fire departments have endorsed me, since I've worked with them to improve safety and reduce crime. The other candidates aren't as focused on these things." She angled her head back, and Ariana followed her gaze. At the far end of the street was another group visiting booths and shaking hands.

Aaah, the other candidate for mayor, thought Ariana, squinting her eyes to catch a glimpse of who it was.

"Well, it was lovely to meet you," said Ana, moving on with her entourage. "Don't forget to vote on the first Tuesday of November."

"I liked her," said Nasreen, and Sara *Khala* nodded in agreement.

"Here's the man she's running against," whispered Shams. "He's a good guy too—his name is Ronald, Ronald Hammersmith."

The name rang a bell in Ariana's mind—then she remembered the day she'd been in the garage, the day after they'd first learned about Pamir Market. Uncle Shams and her father had been talking outside, and she'd overheard her uncle mention that he'd gone to meet Ronald, who sat on the city's zoning board. Ronald had been sympathetic to the fact that a similar store was opening within the same plaza, but since their lease didn't have a non-compete clause, he'd told them that Lucinda could rent to whoever she wanted. *And that meant the stinking Ghilzais moved in.*

"We'll have to hear what he has to say too," said Nasreen.

Within minutes Ronald was at the booth next door, chatting with the petite gray-haired vendor selling brightly painted pottery. Ariana eyed his casual attire—jeans and a Windbreaker, the complete opposite of his opponent, Ana Cardoso. With his long reddish hair tied back in a ponytail, he looked more like a surfer than a candidate for mayor.

"Smart urban renewal is very important for our city," Ronald explained to the potter. "If we invest in renovating our shopping districts and bring in new restaurants and lovely businesses such as yours, Fremont will become a tourist destination."

"Why, thank you," the woman said, and blushed. "I've been looking for a nice location to expand my business, but it's been difficult."

"Well, as mayor I can change that," Ronald said, smiling. "I bring twenty years of real estate development experience coupled with a dedication to environmental responsibility. I'm convinced that with sustained land development we can keep Fremont prosperous and green. Both the Chamber of Commerce and the League of Small Businesses support my platform."

A muscular young man in crisp khakis and a crew cut paused at Ronald's elbow and whispered something into his ear. As Ronald listened, Ariana blinked at a memory that flared in the back of her mind. She eyed Ronald's reddish hair and recalled that she'd seen him before but couldn't put her finger on when or where. Then again, his image was all over town— on posters, in the newspaper, and on local television shows. Before she could think further, his assistant pivoted and disappeared into the crowd. Another one of Ronald's assistants, a willowy woman with silvery blond hair and a bright smile, stepped forward to chat with Nasreen, breaking Ariana's line of sight. The woman handed her mother a leaflet, which Nasreen slipped into the money box next to Ana's. They began to talk, just as Zayd tugged Ariana's hair to get her attention.

"Hey, Ari, we're totally running low on almond cookies and the rose petal jam. Can you and Laila run back to the truck and get the last box?"

Ariana frowned. She wanted to stay and find out what Ronald had to say.

"Look, I would have made the twins do it, or Baz, but they've all disappeared."

Laila, always agreeable, opened her mouth, but Ariana gave her a look to be quiet. She wasn't about to do her brother a favor without getting anything in return. She folded her arms across her chest and raised her eyebrow at him.

"Okay, I get it," said Zayd. "Look, after you come back, I'll take over the booth and you and Laila can go have some fun."

"Okay," agreed Ariana with a satisfied grin.

Laila followed Ariana as she made her way past the food pavilion toward the parking lot. Shadows lengthened along the ground, indicating that dusk was a few short hours away.

"Well, at least we can *finally* have some fun soon," said Ariana, a spring in her step.

"I've never been to a fair like this," said Laila, her eyes wide, staring at a man contorting and twisting a long balloon into a bunny shape. "I hope we can see some of the performances."

"Me too," said Ariana, feeling lighthearted for the first time in a long time.

They paused a moment to admire a display of crystal earrings, then wandered past a clothing stall to their reliable beige truck. As they lugged the box of jam back to their booth, they spotted Hava Bibi.

"*Salaam alaikum,* girls," Hava Bibi said as Zayd took the box.

"*Walaikum a'salaam,*" responded the girls, hurrying to join her.

Zayd took over the booth, and the trio wandered

into the food pavilion to grab something to eat. Hava Bibi bought them frozen chocolate-covered bananas, and they strolled past stalls selling handmade candles, mosaics, and recycled handbags made out of old jeans. As Ariana took the last bite of her banana, they reached the second stage, where they stopped to watch a performance of *bharata natyam*, a classical south Indian dance. Three girls in elaborate silk saris and jewelry, and with marigolds in their hair, moved their bodies into intricate positions, accompanied by a troupe of tabla and sitar players.

As Ariana, Laila, and their grandmother moved to occupy one of the free tables, Hava Bibi's steps faltered and she reached out to grab a chair.

"Are you okay?" asked Laila, taking Hava Bibi's arm.

Hava Bibi nodded, but her face had gone pale, matching the creamy whiteness of her headscarf. She looked as if she'd seen a ghost.

Ariana saw an old man striding toward them, leaning heavily on a cane. The man was dressed in dapper gray trousers, a white shirt, and a tweed coat, and his silver hair was combed back and set with pomade. His bright blue eyes were focused like lasers on her grandmother. As if that weren't jarring enough, right behind him was Wali, who glowered when he spotted Ariana.

"Hava, is that you?" called out the old man, his voice raspy.

Two spots of pink appeared on Hava Bibi's cheeks. "Oh my goodness. Tofan, is that *you*?"

Tofan. The name started bells ringing in Ariana's head. *This is the man my great-grandfather shot.*

"Yes, it's me," said Tofan. "After all these years, how are *you*?"

"Fine . . . just fine," said Hava Bibi, flustered. "And you? What about Dilshad?"

"I'm in good health and so is Dilshad," he said with a twinkle in his eye. "She lives in London and has eight grandchildren."

"You must give me her phone number," said Hava Bibi with a wistful smile. "I do so miss my old friend."

"But of course," said Tofan. "Do you remember how you girls got stuck on Kunar River when my sister had the bright idea of taking out our father's old boat?"

Hava Bibi laughed, her face lighting up. "Yes, I remember. My goodness—we had no idea the boat had a huge hole! We would have drowned if you hadn't swum out and pulled us back to shore!"

What's going on? thought Ariana, exchanging a guarded look with Laila, who clutched a melting banana. *Why is Hava Bibi being so friendly to a Ghilzai?*

Remembering the horse meat flyers, Ariana stiffened, her gaze colliding with Wali's. He looked as surprised as she felt, and conflicting emotions of anger and confusion flitted across his face.

"How is your leg?" asked Hava Bibi, her brows knitted in concern.

"It bothers me only on rainy days," he said with a laugh. Then his handsome features crinkled with worry. "You must know what is going on between the boys. It's just like it was back in Afghanistan. It's madness."

"Yes, yes, I know," replied Hava Bibi. "I told my sons that the feud between our fathers was left behind in Afghanistan. I convinced my eldest, Jamil, to welcome your nephew to the plaza."

"I told Gulbadin about the feud as well," said Tofan, "and advised him to be friendly toward your sons."

"Well, it seemed like things were okay, at first," said Hava Bibi, frowning. "But then our baker, Haroon, left to work at your nephew's store. It was then that things got tense and the rumors of the feud started up."

Tofan lowered his eyes, appearing a little guilty. "I'm afraid that was my fault."

"What do you mean?" prodded Hava Bibi.

"An old family friend was visiting last month, and we took him to Kandahar Kebob House. He started swapping stories from the old days, and soon everyone in the restaurant knew about the Shinwari-Ghilzai feud and that darn mangy goat. They all thought it was hilarious, and one thing led to another, and it's become a tasty bit of gossip floating around town."

Hava Bibi gave him a stern look, then sighed. "Well, what's done is done. But now the boys are arguing about those silly flyers. Honestly, I can't make head nor tail of it."

"Neither can I," said Tofan. "Gulbadin always respects and listens to me, but out of stubborn pride he won't meet with your sons to resolve the situation."

Surprised, Ariana shared a confused look with Wali.

Just as Hava Bibi was about to say something else, they heard the high-pitched timber of a familiar voice. It was Uncle Shams, and he was headed this way. Tofan and Ariana's grandmother exchanged a knowing look, and he and Wali melted back into the crowd.

That night, when they returned home, Jamil asked Ariana to take the money box to the garage and bring him the cash. He wanted to make a deposit at the bank so that the money wouldn't be lying around the house. Ariana knew the drill. She lugged the box to the garage and twisted the key in the old, temperamental lock. She gave it a quick jiggle, and it popped open. As she put the money, mostly twenties, into the money bag, she couldn't help but think back to the strange meeting at the fair. It seemed like her grandmother and Wali's great-uncle knew each other really well, which had surprised her and Wali both.

After scooping out all the change, Ariana found a bunch of flyers at the bottom of the box. They were the political leaflets her mother and Sara *Khala* had collected from the various political candidates who had been making their rounds at the fair. She spotted Ana's name on a pale blue flyer. Beneath it was Ronald's smiling face on a beautiful shade of viridian green. The bold headline on his campaign flyer promised to bring "Change with Conscience." There were words such as "environmental responsibility," "sustainable urban renewal," and "land management." Not knowing whether her mom wanted to keep them or not, she left them stacked on the corner of the desk. Before Ariana left the garage, she absentmindedly drew another *X* on her calendar.

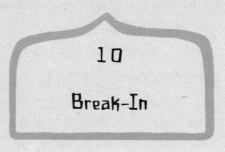

10

Break-In

ARIANA CAME FACE-TO-FACE WITH Wali as she exited language arts class. He was leaning against the lockers, holding the collection box for Kids in Need. She was on her way to meet Josh to work on their Egypt project, and her thoughts were focused on how to convince her obtuse partner that they should build a model pyramid of Giza. Before Ariana could pivot and turn away from Wali, she was propelled toward him, buffeted by the stream of kids scrambling to get to their next class. In a desperate move to escape, she stumbled, but before she landed on her butt, Wali grabbed her arm. After steadying her, he pulled her toward the lockers.

"Are you okay?" he asked, jerking away his hand as if she'd bite it.

"Uh, thanks," said Ariana. "I'm fine." As she looked into his chocolate-brown eyes, she saw them brimming with uncertainty, a feeling of confusion that mirrored her own. For a split second she was tempted to talk to him about the horse meat flyers and her suspicions, but her tongue stayed glued to the roof of her mouth.

Wali opened his lips to say something, but his name rang out through the hall.

"Wali," trilled a high-pitched feminine voice, "is that *bully* bothering you?"

It was Patty and her crew, standing by the water fountain.

Wali reddened. "No, we're just talking."

"I've got to go . . . work on my project," mumbled Ariana, thinking of Josh waiting for her in the library. With a last glance in his direction, she stalked past the water fountain, ignoring Patty's disdainful look. As the distance between her and Wali widened, she couldn't help but feel like she'd missed an important opportunity. The rest of the day she kept an eye out for him, hoping she'd get the nerve to talk to him, but the chance never came.

. . .

"Ari, there was a massacre in Nanger Khel," whispered Laila, leaning toward her on the kitchen table. Laila's daily routine had her glued to the Internet after school, scouting the latest news on Afghanistan. Her father was back at work, making his rounds with American troops, and she was counting the days till he was done.

Ariana blinked in alarm as Laila continued. "The Polish army bombed a village called Nanger Khel, in *badal* for the death of their soldier in Gardez."

"In *badal*?" whispered Ariana, the dumpling in her hand forgotten.

"Yes," replied Laila. "When they shelled the village, many civilians were killed—a pregnant woman and children, including a baby."

"That's awful," said Ariana, aghast.

"What are you two whispering about?" asked Hava Bibi, taking a pot of homemade yogurt from the fridge. "Did I hear 'Gardez'?"

Laila nodded as Ariana got busy crimping the homemade dumplings. They were helping Hava Bibi make *aushak*, a kind of ravioli filled with leeks and spices. After Laila dropped spoonfuls of the leek mixture into wonton wrappers, Ariana then pinched the sides together to make a dumpling. It would then be steamed and drizzled with meat sauce and yogurt.

Hava Bibi paused, a thoughtful look on her face. "My father used to travel to Gardez for business at the Bazar-e Kohna, the old bazaar. He once brought back an ancient Greek coin for me."

"There were Greeks in Afghanistan?" asked Ariana, dumplings again forgotten.

"Oh, yes," said Hava Bibi. "The writing on the coin translated to 'the Victorious.'"

"It was the Greek king, Antimachus II Nikephoros," said Laila. "He was called 'the Victorious' because he ruled all the way from the Hindu Kush to present-day India."

"Smart girl," said Hava Bibi, and Ariana had to agree. "Well," reminisced their grandmother with a frown, "Gardez was also home to Najibullah—the last Soviet-backed president of Afghanistan. He was hanged by the Taliban when they came to power in 1996."

Ariana winked at Laila, who hid a smile; a history lesson was coming.

Hava Bibi leaned against the counter with a frown. "Even though Najibullah was a communist puppet, that's no way to treat a human being. It's a shame that all the changes King Zahir Shah brought to Afghanistan in the 1960s didn't stick," she added. "What did they teach you about him at the *lycée*, Laila?"

"Our teacher told us that the king instituted the first constitution, turning Afghanistan into a democracy. He formed a parliament that established civil rights for all Afghans, in particular for women."

"That's right," said Hava Bibi with a sad sigh. "When Jamil was nearly four years old, we had our first elections in Afghanistan. But sadly, the king made a terrible mistake."

"What?" Ariana blurted out. Her parents didn't talk about Afghan history, and it wasn't anything the teachers in the United States ever covered in school.

"As the government set up modern industries, they accepted aid from the Soviet Union, the same country that would invade them two decades later, and depose Zahir Shah as the last king. Then, when the Soviets realized they could never subjugate the Afghan people, they fled, leaving Najibullah, who ended up hanging from a light pole. But in the end who suffers?" muttered Hava Bibi. "It's the common people, that's who. Years of war have brought nothing but poverty, illiteracy, sickness, and death."

"Oh," said Ariana in a small voice. It was because of the Soviet invasion that her family had left Afghanistan in the first place.

The phone rang, interrupting the conversation.

Ariana wiped her hands on a kitchen towel and picked it up. "This is Officer Nguyen with the Fremont Police Department," said a deep voice. "Can I speak to Jamil Shinwari, please?"

"Uh, sure," said Ariana, a trickle of dread oozing through her. "Hold on. Let me get him." *What do the police want with Dad?*

Ariana hurried toward the garage, where her father was working on an endless pile of paperwork.

"It's for you," she whispered, handing him the phone. "It's a policeman," she added, stepping aside, hoping he wouldn't send her away.

"This is Jamil Shinwari," said her father, seeming to forget that she was even there. Ariana watched her father's face go pale as he clutched the phone to his ear. "Oh, no!" he exclaimed.

Ariana's heart rammed against her rib cage. *What happened?*

"How much damage?" asked Jamil. He paused for a few minutes, listening. "I'll be right there." He hung up and dialed another number. "Shams, it's me,

Jamil," he said in a rush. "Meet me at the store as soon as you can—it's urgent."

He jumped up from his chair and headed into the house, with Ariana at his heels. He shouted up the stairs for Zayd and grabbed the car keys sitting on the hall table.

"What's up, Dad?" asked Zayd, hurrying downstairs.

"Just come with me," said Jamil, his usually controlled voice cracking.

"Sure," said Zayd, grabbing a coat.

"I want to come," said Ariana, expecting her father to say no. But to her surprise he just nodded, running a distracted hand through his hair as he dashed out of the house.

Officer Nguyen and his partner stood beside their squad car, its red-and-blue lights flashing in the empty plaza. Jamil pulled in next to them and ordered Ariana and Zayd to remain in the car. Ariana managed to lower the window a bit before her father turned off the ignition and leapt out.

"Mr. Shinwari?" asked Officer Nguyen as her father hurried over.

"Yes, I'm Jamil Shinwari. What happened?"

"We were called to the scene by a Mr. Martinez, proprietor of Juan More Tacos. As Mr. Martinez was closing up, he noticed that the door to your store was wide open. He investigated and then called 911."

Zayd gave Ariana a worried look. "What's going on?" he whispered.

"I don't know any more than you do," replied Ariana. Neither of them had uttered a word during the tense six-minute drive to Wong Plaza, nor had they asked their obviously agitated father any questions.

The officers and Jamil walked into Kabul Corner as one of the policemen took notes. After what seemed like a good half hour, the police left the store and drove away, leaving Jamil inside. Fidgety from being cooped up in the car, Zayd couldn't take it anymore. He hopped out of the backseat, with Ariana right behind him. They scurried toward the door of the store, which gaped open.

Ariana peered inside, spotting an overturned spice rack lying across the entrance. The ground was streaked with cumin, dried mint, cinnamon, and red pepper.

"What the—," whispered Zayd, his face going pale.

Ariana's throat tightened as she surveyed the

store; it looked like an IED had exploded inside. She blinked, not believing what she saw. The cash register lay a few feet from the counter where it had been yanked from the wall. The new freezer's doors hung drunkenly agape, and the new line of frozen kebobs, melting and turning into mush, were on the floor next to overturned nut bins. Everywhere she looked was destruction—torn packaging and broken glass lay strewn in the aisles; the contents of shattered jars littered the linoleum; jams oozed and mixed with pickles, olives, and tomato sauce.

"Oh, no," whispered Ariana, shivering.

Zayd reached out and slipped an arm around her shoulders in a protective hug. She stood there, huddling next to her brother's warmth, as they stared at their father. Jamil picked up the cash register, tears gleaming in his eyes. Then he paused, seemingly immobilized by the carnage before him. Ariana sunk deeper into shock. She'd never seen her father cry, except when Masood *Baba*, her grandfather, had lain dying at the hospital.

"Who did this?" Zayd whispered out loud.

"They don't know," said Jamil. "Juan found the store like this and called the cops."

As they stood at the front of the store, surveying the

damage, Uncle Shams's minivan screeched to a halt outside. He tumbled out with Baz and Marjan trailing behind. "Oh my goodness," he said with a gasp as he viewed the destruction. "We're ruined!" he cried, deflating against the counter as if someone had let the air out of his body.

Jamil blinked, coming out of his stupor. He glanced at the kids as they stood, wide-eyed with fear. "Now, Shams," he began, his voice ragged but calm. "I know it looks bad, but we can clean this up."

"This is thousands and thousands of dollars' worth of damage," muttered Uncle Shams, looking around in a daze.

"Don't worry," soothed Jamil. "I'll call the insurance company first thing in the morning and file a claim, once I have a copy of the police report."

Uncle Shams sat on a stool behind the counter, holding his head in his hands.

While Zayd called their mom and Sara *Khala*, Ariana and her cousins headed back to the bakery, which was covered with a layer of flour. All the bags had been slashed and the contents strewn everywhere.

"Man, it looks like snow," said Baz, wielding a broom.

Marjan nodded, his round face crumpling. "Who'd do this?" he whispered.

"Don't worry about that now," said Ariana, giving him an awkward hug. Marjan wrapped his pudgy arms around her and wiped his nose on her shoulder. *Eeeww,* thought Ariana, but she resisted the temptation to shove him off.

Marjan stepped back, a little embarrassed. "C'mon. Let's clean this up."

Ariana returned to the front of the store with garbage bags so that she could start sorting through what could be salvaged and what couldn't. She shut the front door and stood at the window, gazing across the deserted parking lot. Beyond the flickering sign with the missing *g* sat the dilapidated auto parts warehouse, which now had a SOLD sign hanging on it. Someone had finally bought the eyesore.

"Ariana *jaan,*" called her father. "Can you please get us the mops?"

Ariana nodded, stepping over the torn velvet cushions. She held back a gag reflex from the caustic stench of vinegar, mustard, and cayenne pepper swirling together like a witch's brew. Nose held between her fingers, Ariana hurried back to the supply room. Wishing she had some cotton balls to stick in her nose, she pushed open the door and found overturned boxes and supplies.

As she exited, she heard Uncle Shams's angry voice reverberating near the back door. "It was those thieving Ghilzais!"

"Now, Shams . . . ," began Jamil, attempting to hold back his brother's flood of words.

"Of course it's them! All our problems began when they moved in next door. Only they would gain from driving us out of business."

"Don't jump to conclusions, Shams," cautioned Jamil. "The police don't have any clues as to who did this."

Ariana could just imagine her uncle inflated like a puffer fish filled with air. "Until there is proof otherwise, I am convinced that it's those Ghilzais."

Ariana held her breath. Uncle Shams had a habit of getting angry quickly, but she'd never seen him this furious.

Jamil released a pent-up sigh and then remained silent a moment, as if he'd run out of words to convince Shams otherwise. "All right," he said, changing the subject. "For now all of us need to calm down and get this mess cleaned up. But we will get to the bottom of who did this."

11

Connecting Dots

"IT WAS LIKE A bomb had gone off inside the store,"
murmured Ariana, staring morosely at the contents of
her lunch bag.

Mariam's hand stopped in midair, her forkful of
spaghetti dripping crimson sauce onto her crisp
coral-colored shirt. "Was it really *that* bad?"

Ariana nodded, her expression glum. Laila stared
at her midchew; she'd been asleep when Ariana had
returned with Jamil and her brother and cousins at
nearly two a.m. the night before. Since Ariana and
the boys had been allowed to sleep through breakfast, Laila had gotten only tidbits of what had hap-

pened from the adults, and she'd been dying to hear the details.

"How bad is it?" whispered Laila, choking down the bite of sandwich.

"It's pretty bad," said Ariana, rubbing her shoulder, sore from hours of sweeping. "They ripped out the cash register and stole the petty cash. But then they went on a rampage through the store. They destroyed tens of thousands of dollars' worth of inventory. The dry goods—flour, rice, lentils, sugar, and spices—were all torn apart. They shoved jars of pickles, jams, and sauces onto the floor, creating a slippery, toxic sludge. Even Uncle Shams's new line of kebobs were pulled out of the freezer and ended up in a soggy melted mess. We cleaned for, like, five hours, but there's a ton more to do."

"Oh, no," said Mariam, laying down her fork.

"Why didn't they just take the money and leave?" pondered Laila.

Laila's got a point, thought Ariana with a frown. The vandals had taken a risk by hanging out to trash the place. They could have gotten caught.

Laila gulped, her lips compressed. "It's like it was *personal,*" she said. "As if they wanted to destroy not only the store but also Uncle Jamil's and Uncle Shams's spirit."

"Your father and uncle must be devastated," said Mariam.

Ariana nodded, Uncle Shams's words from the night before ringing in her ears. "He thinks the Ghilzais did it."

"It's just like Zia and Bawer," said Laila, sharing a worried look with Ariana.

"Who and who?" asked Mariam.

Ariana and Laila filled Mariam in on their family history and the feud that went all the way back to Afghanistan.

"Wow," said Mariam, her eyes wide. "That sounds like those two crazy families we learned about last year, the Garfields and the McDougals."

"The Hatfields and McCoys," corrected Ariana.

"Yeah, them," said Mariam. "They, like, killed off half of each other's family."

"Do you think Uncle Shams will get mad enough to retaliate against them?" wondered Laila out loud.

Ariana shivered. "I've never seen him so mad. He's convinced the Ghilzais had something to do with the break-in. He's like a rumbling volcano that's going to explode at any minute."

"You never know what can happen if someone is pushed to the edge," whispered Laila, and she nudged aside the rest of her sandwich, her appetite gone. "Remember how one tiny incident with the goat escalated into a cycle of *badal* and kept getting worse until Tofan *Baba* was shot? What if the police don't find proof of who broke into the store and Uncle Shams takes the law into his own hands . . ." Her words trailed off, but the girls knew what she was thinking.

What if Uncle Shams gets mad enough to do something to Gulbadin?

"Well, if the Ghilzais really did break in, they should be brought to justice before Uncle Shams takes the law into his own hands," said Mariam.

Ariana exchanged a secretive look with Laila. "But that's just it, Mariam. . . . We don't think that the Ghilzais did it."

"Why in the world would you think that?" asked her friend. "They have every reason to want you guys out of business."

"It's an odd feeling I have," said Ariana. "Some of what's happened just doesn't add up."

"What do you mean?" asked Mariam.

"Let me try to explain," said Ariana, sorting it out in her own mind first. "It all started when the Ghilzais opened Pamir Market across from us.

Although that wasn't cool of them, it wasn't like it was illegal—and it wasn't against the rules in Mrs. Wong's lease. Uncle Shams looked into that and found out that the lease doesn't have something called a non-compete clause, meaning there can be a competing business in the same plaza."

"That stinks," said Mariam, wrinkling her nose.

"Yeah, I know," said Ariana. "Then Pamir Market had its grand opening and we found out that they'd cut their prices to attract more customers."

"That must have made your father and uncle mad," said Mariam.

"Yeah, but that's not illegal either," explained Ariana. "It was when Haroon left and ended up at Pamir Market that the problems, and the gossip, really began."

Mariam nodded. She'd heard the rumors flying around, from her parents. "Does anyone know how they stole Haroon from you guys?" she asked.

"No. Dad and Uncle Shams have been too busy trying to figure out a way to get back customers and bring in more money," said Ariana. She remembered her parents huddled in the kitchen, whispering about using the kids' college fund to help cover expenses.

"Maybe we should just ask Haroon," suggested Laila.

Ariana nodded, though the thought of going behind her father's back to talk to their old baker made her a little nervous. "Okay," she said, inspired to do a little digging. "Let's put that on a to-do list."

Laila pulled out her notebook and opened to a clean page. On the top she wrote *Feud Investigation*. Next to number one she wrote, *Talk to Haroon*.

"Then, a couple of weeks later, the horse meat flyers appeared out of thin air," said Ariana. "And I know that Dad and Uncle Shams didn't have anything to do with them."

"But we did benefit from Pamir Market's bad publicity," said Laila. "A lot of our old customers came back."

"For a while Dad thought the Ghilzais had put the flyers up so they could accuse us of harassing them," said Ariana. "But as Laila and I examined the flyer, we realized that that made no sense. Why would they damage the reputation of their own store? The more we analyzed the flyer, the more questions we had."

"Yes," said Laila. "We translated the Farsi into English, and the wording of the flyer is terrible. It sounds like it wasn't even written by a Farsi-speaking person."

"But that's not *real* proof that the Ghilzais didn't do it," said Mariam.

"You're right." Ariana sighed. "So, we need solid evidence, whether the Ghilzais are involved or it's someone else."

Laila wrote, *Find proof whether Ghilzais are behind the flyer.*

"So Uncle Shams believes that the break-in was the Ghilzais' way of getting back at you for the flyers?" asked Mariam.

"Yeah," said Ariana, her shoulders slumping. Her father and Uncle Shams were still in the process of cleaning out the store and haggling with the insurance company about getting payment for the losses.

"But the police don't have any suspects or proof, right?" asked Mariam.

"Yup," said Ariana. "They think it could have been anyone—maybe a bunch of teenagers out for some fun, making trouble."

"Maybe the door was left unlocked," said Mariam.

"No." Ariana frowned. "My dad and Uncle Shams are supercareful about locking up, especially these days."

Mariam looked thoroughly confused. "But who else can it be?"

The two cousins shrugged.

"There's only one way to uncover the answers to these questions," said Mariam, looking Ariana in the eye. "You know what we have to do, right?"

Ariana gulped. *Man, this is going to be hard.*

Three hours later, lodged behind a bush next to the gym, Ariana and Laila watched Mariam standing under the monkey bars with Wali. A splash of coral against the dull, gray October afternoon, Mariam bent toward him, hands on hips, her face earnest. Wali stood with his hands in his pockets, nodding, then shaking his head. As the neutral party, Mariam had been tasked with talking to him. So she'd had a friend give Wali a note during math, asking him to meet her after school on the playground. Ariana kept her fingers crossed. She had no idea how this was going to go.

But five minutes later Mariam came running toward them at their appointed meet-up spot, outside the gym door. "It's on," she trilled. "Four o'clock at the Fremont library."

• • •

"I swear on my honor—my father didn't lure Haroon away from your store," said Wali. His fists clenched, he leaned across the table and stared at the girls.

They were on the second floor of the library, in a secluded spot between the travel books and cookbooks.

"How can you be so sure?" prodded Mariam, looking him dead in the eye.

"Haroon came to our house," said Wali, pushing back a lock of hair. "My father had never even thought of having a bakery at the store. Honestly, he was out of money. He'd spent thousands to upgrade Pamir Market for the grand opening."

"So Haroon just showed up?" asked Ariana, trying to keep the incredulity out of her voice. She'd been quiet so far, picking at the red and green paint stuck under her fingernails from painting *Peter Pan* sets.

"Yes. Haroon said he'd had it with the Shinwari brothers, the awful ovens, and the terrible assistant. He said he needed a change, and more pay. My father thought it was too good an opportunity to pass up, so he sold his BMW to put a bakery at the back of the store, and hired Haroon."

Well, that did sound like something Haroon would say and do, thought Ariana grudgingly.

"Look," said Wali. "When Mariam told me that you

wanted to talk about what was happening between the stores, I took a risk to come here. If my dad found out I was talking to you, he'd be furious. He'd ground me for a year. But you know what, with all the weird stuff going on, something just doesn't *feel* right."

Startled, Ariana tried to gauge the sincerity in Wali's face, wondering at his choice of words. It didn't *feel* right to her, either. "Well, the news is out that our stores are feuding," she growled, drumming her fingers against the table.

"Look," said Wali, sounding exasperated. "My father didn't even *know* about the feud in Afghanistan until Tofan *Baba* told us."

"So where did the idea of the feud come from?" pushed Mariam, like she was interrogating someone on the witness stand.

"That was Tofan *Baba*'s friend's fault," muttered Wali, squirming in his chair.

Ariana remembered the conversation Hava Bibi and Tofan *Baba* had had at the festival. "Didn't his friend tell everyone at the kebob restaurant about Zia, Bawer, and the goat?"

"Yeah," said Wali, "but Tofan *Baba* told them it wasn't like that in America—that the old feud had been left behind in Afghanistan."

"But the story *is* out," said Mariam. "My dad said he heard some guys talking about it at the mosque the other week."

"But that's how gossip works," said Ariana. "After Haroon left for Pamir Market, the whole world began to believe that our stores are fighting."

"That's why we need to go through this list," said Mariam, pointing to Laila's notebook. "We need to understand all the facts and find out what's really going on."

"What's on your list?" asked Wali, leaning back in his chair, arms folded across his chest.

Laila looked at the Feud Investigation list and read out, "Mystery meat flyers."

"My dad was furious when he saw those," said Wali. "He's totally convinced that your family put them up."

Ariana pulled the yellow flyer with the ink smudges from her backpack and laid it in front of Wali. "My family had *nothing* to do with these," she said, her voice gruff. She explained how the flyers had been printed on expensive paper, and if her father had been behind it, *which he hadn't been*, he wouldn't have wasted money on good paper.

"Then who did it?" asked Wali.

"Now, that is the million-dollar question," said Mariam.

"Uh, what is a million-dollar question?" asked Laila.

That got a smile out of the three, and Mariam explained that it was another American saying that meant it was an important or difficult question that people didn't know the answer to.

"Oh," said Laila. "Well, the last item on the list is also a million-dollar question. *Who vandalized Kabul Corner?*"

"I'll swear again," said Wali, raising his hands. "We had nothing to do with that. We were having a family dinner last night, and everyone stayed at the house until well past nine o'clock."

"Well, if your family didn't do it, then according to the police it was a bunch of teenagers, destroying property for fun," said Mariam.

"I don't know," said Ariana. "Even though Wong Plaza has gotten kind of run-down over the years, it's always been a safe place."

"There's always that first time," said Wali with a shrug.

Laila picked up the flyer, a contemplative look on her face. "What if someone else is pitting the two families against each other?" she ventured.

Ariana sat up in surprise.

The question got Wali's attention and he paused, eyes wide. "That makes sense in an odd sort of way," he said. "If neither of our families put up those flyers or vandalized your store, then someone else must have done it."

Mariam took the flyer from Laila. "Look, the purpose of the flyer is to ruin Pamir Market's reputation, and we know that neither family had anything to do with it. But, although it's an important clue, it's circumstantial."

"What's circumstantial?" asked Laila and Ariana at the same time.

"Well, I've watched enough episodes of *Unlawful Conduct* to know that the horse meat flyers are like fingerprints. Fingerprints found at the scene of a crime can confirm that someone was present but they don't necessarily prove that they did anything illegal."

"Oh," said Laila, still looking a little confused.

"We need to prove our hypothesis that someone else is behind the feud by finding *direct evidence—*

concrete proof—that a mysterious third party is behind the whole thing."

"That's the key," said Wali. "We need to know *who* it was and *why* they did it."

"Now, that really is the billion-dollar question," said Mariam.

Laila flipped the page of her notebook and started another list titled *Potential Suspects*.

"Who would benefit from the stores being shut down?" pondered Mariam.

They sat around looking at one another, unable to come up with a name.

"How about your landlady?" asked Mariam, throwing out a name.

Ariana frowned, remembering the look of worry on Mrs. Wong's face when she'd come into Kabul Corner after the horse meat flyers had gone up. "I don't think she could be behind this," she said. "When she came into the store after the flyers went up, she was really upset."

Wali nodded. "She was really happy when my dad signed the lease to open Pamir Market."

"Yeah," said Ariana, remembering her father and uncle talking about Hooper's Diner. "She doesn't want any of the stores in Wong Plaza shutting down. She'll lose a lot of rent."

"Okay," said Mariam. "Who else? We really need to brainstorm here."

"How about the other store owners?" said Wali, warming up to the task.

"We've known them for years," said Ariana. "Why would they do something like this?"

"It's hard to know anyone's motives," said Mariam.

"Yeah," said Wali. "Maybe someone wants your store because it has the best location."

Ariana reluctantly nodded. They did have the biggest store on the plaza, at the best location, anchored on the west end of the strip. She'd once overheard Mr. Milan telling her father that he would love to have more space to add a line of teak furniture at the Emporium.

So they added to the list Juan Martinez, Gopal and Neela Milan, Soo Min Koo, and Harold and Minerva Smith.

"Who else could want the stores out of business?" pushed Mariam.

"Well, we can add the new owner of the Beadery Bead Shoppe, and Mr. Hooper."

"But Hooper's Diner shut down," said Mariam.

"He had a heart attack," Ariana added. "He's retired and living with one of his sons—I think he's a lawyer and lives in Palo Alto, on the other side of the bay."

"Doesn't hurt to list him," said Wali.

"Oh, there was a woman," said Ariana, remembering. "Leslie something or other, who was interested in our store. She wanted to turn it into a pizza joint."

Laila scribbled her name down too. Ten minutes later, while Laila jotted down the last of their notes, Ariana glanced at Wali from under her eyelashes. Reservations still plagued her, but she realized that if they were going to be a team, she had to trust him. Wali looked up and caught her staring; he gave her a slight nod, and she returned it. It was a done deal. They were in this together and they needed to solve the mystery of who was trying to drive their stores out of business, before something else bad happened.

The foursome collected their things and disbanded, exhausted. After much thought they'd decided not to tell the grown-ups about their suspicions. Wali had said it best. "Do you really think our parents are going to believe us? They'll think we're nuts if we tell them that someone else is trying to make it look like our families are feuding." The others had agreed and decided to keep their lips zipped. Besides, their parents were constantly preoccupied these days—worried about the feud, their families and financial uncertainty. Telling the grown-ups about their suspicions would freak them out, and they would probably order the kids to stop snooping around and wasting their time. Stopping was something they couldn't do—the strange clues were begging them to uncover the truth.

12

Twisty Turns

THE ONE PERSON ARIANA was dying to tell was Hava Bibi. After seeing her grandmother and Tofan *Baba* together at the fair, she thought that those two would take the kids seriously. After she and Laila got ready for bed that night, they headed downstairs for milk and cookies, hoping to talk to their grandmother. On their way down the phone rang, and Laila tensed, as she usually did when the shrill sound reverberated through the house. Ariana looked at her and gave her what she hoped was a calming smile.

"Hello?" said Jamil. After a minute he said, "And you are certain?" A long pause followed. "Yes, Sergeant

Maxwell, I will convey the message to her."

The girls stood, transfixed, a worried look spreading across Laila's face as she clutched the locket at her throat. *Getting a call from the army doesn't sound good,* thought Ariana, and she gave Laila's hand a comforting squeeze.

They reached the bottom of the stairs as Jamil hurried out of the kitchen, rounded the corner, and disappeared into the garage, while calling out, "Mother, Nasreen, Zainab, please come into the garage."

"What's going on?" whispered Laila, her eyes a stormy jade.

"Don't worry. We'll find out," said Ariana.

They were sitting in silence, dipping their cookies in milk, when they heard Nasreen call them into the living room ten minutes later. The adults were sitting against the cushions, their faces drawn.

"What happened?" Ariana burst out, not able to contain her growing anxiety.

Laila crept over to sit between her mother and Hava Bibi, while Ariana stood.

"It's your father, *jaan.* He's . . . ," began Zainab *Khala*, her voice breaking.

Hava Bibi gently interrupted while hugging Laila. "There was battle near Jalalabad," she said, her voice oddly upbeat. "You father's battalion came across a group of Taliban soldiers, and during the fight Hamza got separated from the rest of his troops."

"But they found him, right?" asked Laila.

"No, sweetheart," said Zainab *Khala*, wiping her eyes with her shawl. "They did a perimeter search, but they haven't found him yet."

"Is he . . . dead?" whispered Laila.

"No, no . . . ," said Nasreen, trailing off.

Ariana knew what she meant. *If Uncle Hamza was dead, they'd have found his body.*

"Sergeant Maxwell is very hopeful that he'll be found soon," said Jamil. "They think Hamza has found a hiding spot, and when things calm down, he'll find his way back."

"Now, I know you cannot help but worry," said Hava Bibi. "But pray to Allah that he returns safe and unharmed."

Laila nodded, her movements jerky.

"I'm going to make some phone calls," said Jamil. "Maybe some of our friends have contacts in that area that can help."

The women got up to make tea, and Ariana, not knowing how to make Laila feel better, grabbed her hand and guided her into the garage. They'd do something that always calmed Ariana down.

"Maybe he was taken hostage," muttered Laila.

"Don't think the worst," Ariana said, patting Laila's back as she settled her at her father's desk.

As she reached for the origami box, her gaze fell on her calendar. Ariana had been preoccupied with the worried looks her parents, aunt, and uncle had been exchanging when they thought the kids weren't looking. Both families had been quietly cutting costs—fewer trips, to cut down on gas; no more fancy purchases or visits to the movies; and the thermostat was set to a lower temperature to save on electricity. She'd even heard Uncle Shams whisper the dreaded word "bankruptcy," but her father had quickly shushed him up.

Ariana examined the line of bright red Xs that stopped on October 16. A line of empty white boxes stretched into the future, and the image of her room shimmered before her, slowly fading beyond her reach. It looked more and more likely that her father would forfeit their deposit on the new house, if he hadn't done so already. They were struggling to survive; there was no extra money for the mortgage. There would be no new house. There would be no new room. Stamping down the urge to rip the calendar off the wall and feel sorry for herself, Ariana focused on what Laila must have been going through. It was just a house. She couldn't even imagine her father being missing. She grabbed her origami box and extracted two sheets of six-by-six inch duo paper, bright red on one side and pale pink on the other. She rubbed a crisp sheet soothingly between her fingers, feeling the lightweight paper practically float in her hand.

"Come on. I want to show you how to make a cherry blossom," she told her cousin, trying to make her voice upbeat.

Laila looked a bit dazed, but took the page as if it were a lifeline.

Ariana turned on the radio, and soon the garage was filled with the sounds of bouncy pop music. "Look here," she said, pointing to a page in the origami book.

With the red side up she showed Laila how to fold the paper in half on the horizontal axis and make a nice crease. The next step involved creating an X crease, but she needed a ruler to make sure it was precise. She opened the left-hand drawer, looking for her father's office supplies, but instead she found a stack of files. On the edge she caught the words "Police Report: Kabul Corner."

Without thinking, she pulled it out and laid it

under the lamp. Most of the first page contained official details, such as the police officers' badge numbers, the location of the store, and the time the incident was reported. The details from the crime scene filled the following pages. On page two Ariana saw Officer Nguyen's notes, and the first line of the second paragraph leapt out at her.

We found no sign of forcible entry into the store . . .

She frowned, not fully understanding what that meant. Then she continued reading. At the bottom was written, *The front store windows were broken from the inside out, as we can see from the pattern of glass shards radiating out onto the sidewalk.*

"Laila," whispered Ariana. "Look at this."

Her cousin looked away from the origami book. "What is it?"

"The officer wrote that the front door of the store was not forced open."

"What do you mean?" asked Laila.

"Someone went through the front door without breaking it open. They couldn't have gone through the front windows, since they were broken from the inside out, not the other way around."

"Do you think your father or Uncle Shams accidentally left the door open?"

"I don't know. . . . Father and Uncle Shams are so careful about closing up these days."

"Who else has a key to the store?"

"The only other person, besides my father and Uncle Shams, is Mrs. Wong, our landlady."

"But we've ruled her out as a suspect," said Laila.

Ariana nodded, but a sense of uncertainty grew inside her. Even though Lucinda didn't benefit from the feud, and actually was harmed by it, she was the only other person with a key to the store.

The next day Wali met Ariana a few blocks down from Wong Plaza. "Are you ready for phase two?" he asked as they began their short walk to Mrs. Wong's house.

"As ready as I'll ever be," Ariana replied. Within a few short minutes they were at Mrs. Wong's door. Before she could knock, Wali stopped her. "Ariana—"

"Call me Ari," she said. "All my friends do."

"Uh, okay," said Wali with a nervous smile. "I just want to say thank you. Thank you for trusting me to work with you guys. I know we didn't get off to a good start, and I wish things were better between our families, and us, but I'm really glad we're doing this together." Then he stuck out his hand toward her.

Ariana stared down at his long fingers with their neatly clipped nails and tentatively shook them. "I'm glad too," she said.

"Okay, then," said Wali, gesturing toward the red peeling door with the brass knocker.

Taking a deep breath, Ariana muttered to Wali, "Keep your eyes open for clues." She knocked on the faded door of the one-story bungalow that served as Mrs. Wong's house and her office.

Mrs. Wong opened the door and gazed at them through bifocals, her black eyes magnified. "Hello, kids. This is a surprise. How can I help you?"

"Good afternoon, Mrs. Wong," said Ariana. "I'm really sorry to bother you, but Wali and I need to ask you a couple of questions."

"Sure, come on in," said Mrs. Wong, opening the door so they could slip inside. "I was just watching *The Price Is Right* with my son. He just loves guessing the prices of those silly prizes. They're competing over a washer and dryer right now."

The kids made their way into the living room and spotted Mrs. Wong's son sitting next to the television screen, rocking back and forth, his hands clasped together. He was forty-three years old but had the exuberance of a kindergartner.

"Hi, Martin," said Ariana. She'd met him many times over the years when he'd accompanied Mrs. Wong to the store.

Martin grinned and waved back, graham cracker crumbs covering the front of his Mickey Mouse T-shirt. "Green nuts?" he said, looking at her expectantly.

Martin loved pistachios, and Ariana would help shell them for him when he visited Kabul Corner.

"I'm sorry, Martin. I didn't bring any," said Ariana. "Next time, I promise." She wished she'd remembered to bring him some, but her mind was overwhelmed with their investigation.

"Take a seat. How about I round us up some lemonade?" asked Mrs. Wong.

As they waited in the living room, Ariana fidgeted on the edge of the sofa, running her hands over the faded nubby fabric, which felt both soft and rough against her palm, heightening her sense of anticipation. Next to her Wali eyed a stack of documents sitting on the coffee table and scooted closer to inspect them. Ariana glanced through the arched doorway, across the hall into the dining room, where a heavy dining table practically groaned under a stack of papers. Behind it hung a corkboard, lined with keys.

Interesting, she thought, noticing that each key was labeled.

To calm her nerves she grabbed a copy of the local paper, the *Tri City Express.* The headline screamed MAYORAL ELECTIONS HEATING UP, and beneath it were pictures of Ronald Hammersmith and Ana Cardoso. A reporter named Terry Yurkovich had written a short article about how the elections were turning personal. Ronald had accused Ana of trying to influence the teachers union with promises to increase school funding. Ana denied the allegation and questioned Ronald's recent land-acquisition deal and his efforts to rezone certain Fremont neighborhoods. It sounded pretty boring to Ariana, who looked over to see that Wali was quickly flipping through the papers, his lips pursed in concentration.

He can't get caught doing that, she thought. Her heart hammered against her ribs. *What if Lucinda comes back suddenly?* She shot over to the arched doorway and positioned herself to watch the hall that led down to the kitchen. But as she glanced into the dining room, she spotted the corkboard with the keys again. Overcome with curiosity, she scurried around the heavy dining table and scrutinized the ten sets of keys hanging in two rows. Pasted above each key was a label with a store name. The first name was Kabul Corner, since it was the store that anchored the west end of the plaza. Next door to it was Juan More Tacos, then Milan's Indian Emporium. The last key on the board was Pamir Market, the last store in the plaza. Each key had a key chain with the corresponding store name. But something was off, and then she saw what it was. The keys for Kabul Corner and Pamir Market had been switched; they hung in the wrong spots. As she reached out to touch them, she heard a creak along the hardwood floor. She shot back across the hall into the living room, clearing her throat loudly to alert Wali that Mrs. Wong was headed back. Wali quickly restacked the sheets and grabbed the cartoon section of the newspaper.

Mrs. Wong sat down with a muffled sigh. "What can I help you kids with?"

Ariana took a big gulp of the too-sweet lemonade and decided to just jump in. "Mrs. Wong, I'm sure you know what happened at our store." She decided to keep mum about the "no forcible entry" bit.

"I know. I feel just terrible about it," said Mrs. Wong, her frown revealing a map of worry lines etched across her face. "The police called me that night, and thankfully, I had my cell phone. I was in

Sacramento visiting my brother and told the police I'd come down first thing in the morning. . . ."

Ariana and Wali exchanged a look. Mrs. Wong had been in Sacramento, a good two-and-a-half-hour drive away, which gave her a valid alibi for that night.

"I really regret not putting in those security cameras," continued Mrs. Wong. "After the break-in I got calls from the other tenants, wanting extra security. I told them that if I had the money, I would gladly do it. But with the state of the economy and with the expense of Martin's care, I'm just plain tapped out."

"We're so sorry to hear about that," said Wali, his voice sincere.

It's now or never, thought Ariana. "So, ummm . . . Mrs. Wong, besides my dad and his brother, are you the only person who has a key to the store?"

"Yes," she said. "I have master keys to all the stores and keep them over there," she said, pointing to the corkboard Ariana had just been examining.

"I see. Well, thank you for your time," said Ariana. "And the lemonade."

"No problem," said Mrs. Wong. "Tell your father if he needs anything from me for the insurance company, let me know. I'm just praying we don't get any more trouble. I don't think my poor heart could take it."

"I will," said Ariana, heading out the door with Wali right behind her. They'd made it halfway down the block when Wali stopped, a guilty look on his face. "Guess what those papers were all about."

"What?" asked Ariana, not in the mood for a game of twenty questions.

"They were all bills," whispered Wali. "Overdue electricity, water, doctor, and credit card bills."

"Oh, no," muttered Ariana, kicking a stray rock off the sidewalk, ashamed to have snooped through Mrs. Wong's personal business.

"I know," said Wali. "She's barely making ends meet, and it looks like she's counting every penny."

"So a problem with tenants at Wong Plaza is the last thing she needs," said Ariana. "She already lost a lot of money when Hooper's Diner closed, so if one of us stopped paying rent, she'd lose even more of her income."

Wali nodded. "She said she was in Sacramento the night of the break-in—so she can't possibly be the culprit."

"I noticed something odd too," said Ariana.

"What?"

"It could be nothing, but given what's been going on, it could mean something."

"Tell me already," insisted Wali.

"Remember the corkboard with all the keys?"

"Yeah, Mrs. Wong pointed it out to us."

"Well, each key was hanging under a label with the store's name. But the keys to Kabul Corner and Pamir Market were switched around."

Wali pursed his lips and blinked a few times. "It could be a simple mistake," he said at last.

"Yeah," said Ariana. "That's probably it."

"It seems really odd, though," he added.

"We'll add it to the list of clues," said Ariana. "But it's still circumstantial, no smoking gun to lead us to the real culprit."

"Yeah," said Wali. "Well, we've just got to keep looking for that direct evidence."

"We need to start investigating the names on our list, then," said Ariana with a drawn-out sigh. *This is going to be a lot of work. . . .*

13

Snooping Around

THE FIRST STORE THEY chose to investigate was Milan's Indian Emporium because of what Mr. Milan had said to Ariana's father, about wanting more space for a line of teak furniture. With the pretense of looking for a shawl for Ariana's mother's birthday, Ariana and Mariam wandered through the emporium, gazing at iridescent jewel-toned saris, sequined fabrics, and costume jewelry. Ariana kept sneezing, her nose tickled by the scent of burning incense as Mrs. Milan helpfully pointed out various options—soft goat-hair pashmina stoles, embroidered woolen throws, and delicate linen shawls worked over with colorful thread.

"Wow, Mrs. Milan," Mariam said with dramatic flair, stroking a turquoise shawl with gold tassels. "You have *so* many beautiful things, but it sure is a little *squished* in here."

"I know." The tiny woman with graying hair and wire-framed glasses sighed. "At one point we thought to move, many years ago. But Lucinda convinced us to stay."

"You could have found a bigger store within the plaza," suggested Ariana, and held her breath.

"True, but we found that this store has good *vaastu shastra*," explained Mrs. Milan.

"What's that?" asked Mariam.

"That means it has a positive cosmic energy that has brought us good luck and many customers. Hopefully that good luck will carry over to someone else one day. My husband and I are getting ready to retire. We've decided to sell the store."

"What do you mean, 'retire'?" Mariam exclaimed, holding her hand against her forehead as if in shock.

Ariana poked her for overacting, and interrupted. "Why would you retire, Mrs. Milan? You've been on the plaza forever."

"Yes, well, that's the point, girls. We've been here forever, and Mr. Milan and I aren't getting any younger. We want to spend more time traveling and enjoying our grandchildren."

Both girls stared at Mrs. Milan in confusion. They hadn't seen this coming at all.

"Oh," said Ariana, saddened by the news. "We're going to miss you."

"We'll still be around, not to worry. This isn't good-bye," replied Mrs. Milan, giving the girls a hug as they left.

"That rules them out," said Mariam, crossing the Milans off their list of potential culprits.

Ariana thought of Mrs. Wong and wondered if she knew that the Milans were leaving. It worried her that it would further reduce Mrs. Wong's rental income if she didn't find a replacement tenant soon.

The next afternoon Ariana dragged Laila to get the chips and salsa that Mr. Martinez had promised them back in September. Ever since Uncle Hamza had gone missing, Laila had taken to hiding out in their room and didn't want to leave the house in case she missed a call from Afghanistan. It had been three days since the call from the army, and there hadn't been any more news about her father; he was still missing but assumed alive.

"You *have* to come with me," Ariana begged.

"You're an important part of this investigation."

"You can do it without me," Laila mumbled.

"But the Shinwari *family* honor is at stake!" Ariana insisted, knowing that her cousin couldn't turn her back on *Pukhtunwali*.

A look of guilt on her face, Laila relented. "Okay, I'll go," she responded.

Ariana gave her a hug and handed her the notebook to take notes, and they headed out to Wong Plaza.

"How is business, Mr. Martinez?" Ariana asked as she and Laila took a seat at the long the counter facing the grill.

Conflicting emotions rippled across Mr. Martinez's tanned face as he ladled out two kinds of piquant salsa. "Well, to be honest, it's slowed down a little," he answered.

"Do you think it has to do with the break-in at our store?" asked Ariana hopefully, an innocent look on her face.

"I feel just awful about what happened," said Mr. Martinez. Then he paused as if to weigh his words. "But it seems that news about the vandalism is out, and there are rumors that Wong Plaza isn't as safe as it used to be."

"I'm afraid to be here after dark," Laila added, hoping Mr. Martinez would say more.

Ariana winked at her and ate a chip loaded with salsa, enjoying the feeling of the jalapeños searing her tongue.

"It's not just you," grumbled Mr. Martinez. "We have customers staying away, and it's been a disaster for business. Lucinda really needs to install those security cameras."

Ariana nodded, remembering Mrs. Wong saying that she didn't have any money for security cameras. *It's true. She really doesn't have the money.*

"It's too bad Fiona wasn't here the night of the break-in," said Mr. Martinez. "She might have seen who it was and called the cops."

"Fiona from the Beadery Bead Shoppe?" asked Ariana. She'd seen Fiona around the plaza; she was kind of hard to miss, with a streak of purple in her hair and chunky jewelry. She'd recently taken over a store next door to Hooper's Diner, which had been a sewing machine repair shop.

"Yes. Her deliveries usually come in late, so she's here most nights, cataloging shipments. But unfortunately, she was in the hospital for a couple of days for back surgery."

Laila chewed on a chip and exchanged a look with Ariana that said *The list of potential culprits is shrinking fast.*

Over the next few days, after drama practice, Ariana and Mariam investigated Well-Read Second-hand Books, lurking in the aisles. They listened to Mr. and Mrs. Smith's endless conversations about random topics, hoping to overhear something that might lead to a breakthrough. As they were about to wrap up their operation one evening, they heard the front door jangle, interrupting the Smiths' debate about the benefits of acupuncture versus homeopathy. It was Mr. Martinez, hoping to purchase some stationery. As he stood at the counter, they started chatting about the break-in at Kabul Corner. The girls huddled in the adjacent aisle, straining to hear every word.

"Well, as luck would have it, I'd returned to my store to pick up some paperwork that night," explained Mr. Martinez. "That's when I saw that the door was wide open. At first I thought Jamil had accidentally left it unlocked, and you can imagine my shock when I went over and saw what had happened."

"Thank goodness you were there and called the police," said Mrs. Smith.

"We have to look after one another," emphasized

Mr. Martinez. "It worries me that the neighborhood is becoming dangerous."

"Very true," said Mrs. Smith. Then she lowered her voice. "I've heard rumors that the Shinwaris and the Ghilzais have it in for each other—some feud that started between the families in the old country."

The girls looked at each other with wide eyes. "How did these lies spread outside the Afghan community?" whispered Ariana, incensed. "It seems like everyone knows about it."

Mariam squeezed Ariana's arm to calm her down so they could listen.

"Now, Minerva, you know that's just gossip," chided her husband

"Personally," said Mr. Martinez, "I think it's a bunch of nonsense. I've known Jamil and Shams more than a decade, and they're good men. I would put money on it that they would never stoop to threatening the Ghilzais over business."

Ariana's heart swelled with affection for Mr. Martinez.

"Well, I know something that's definitely *not* a rumor," said Mrs. Smith, changing the subject. "I was talking to Neela Milan a few days ago, and she heard that Lucinda might be selling Wong Plaza."

"No way!" said Mr. Martinez. "I know Lucinda's had a bit of financial trouble and was approached by a few developers, but she's said no to all of them. Quite frankly, she needs the steady income that the plaza brings in."

"That poor son of hers, Martin, needs an awful lot of care," said Mr. Smith.

"What do you make of the 'Sold' sign on the warehouse?" asked Mr. Martinez.

"I really hope the new owners don't plan on opening up a clunky department store or one of those huge chain bookshops," complained Mr. Smith. "If they do, our little bookshop is going to have some serious competition."

Ariana felt sorry for them. She knew what competition could do to a small business. *Another dead end*, she thought as they snuck out to meet with Wali.

"Well, I picked up my dad's suit at Koo Koo Dry Cleaning," said Wali as they sat at a side table at the Daily Grind.

"What happened?" asked Ariana.

"Mrs. Koo got all teary-eyed and emotional when I mentioned the break-in at your store. She's convinced that a bunch of hooligans are roaming the neighborhood and will attack her store next," he replied.

"She's a very sensitive person," said Ariana, "and gets upset pretty easily."

"You can say that again," said Wali. "Unless she's a really good actress, I don't think she's the culprit."

Ariana and Mariam agreed. They crossed Mrs. Koo's name off the list, which was above the Smiths. They'd put a tiny star next to the Smiths' names after telling Wali what they'd learned. Although the Smiths couldn't be fully crossed off the list, it didn't look like they had a motive for creating the fake feud either.

"We're running out of suspects," murmured Mariam as Ariana and Wali shared a worried look.

She's right, Ariana thought.

Ever since the break-in Uncle Shams had been in a dejected, solemn mood. He was no longer the jovial, boisterous man he used to be, and sometimes when Ariana caught him staring out the store window, toward Pamir Market, her heart would race, remembering his angry words about the Ghilzais. Her father had also taken on a distracted air and was rarely at home.

Even the boys noticed that something was off. Omar knocked on the garage door one night, Hasan lurking behind him, and asked if he could talk to her. They'd overheard their mother and Sara *Khala* whispering that things at the store were getting worse. Surprised that they'd chosen to talk to her and not Zayd, she was truthful. She told them that the family was going through a tough time, but they had to be strong and stick together. After giving her a quick peck on the cheek, they slunk back into the house, leaving Ariana to pore over the folder of clues, trying to piece together something, anything, that might lead her to the culprit behind her family's sorrows.

On the day before Halloween, a quiet afternoon, Uncle Shams closed the store early after receiving a call from Jamil. Seeming more agitated than usual, he dropped Ariana at home, and he and Baz went next door to his own town house. An eerily quiet house greeted Ariana as she entered through the front door, and she headed upstairs, turning on the lights as she went. It looked like no one was home. *Good. I have the whole house to myself,* she thought with a smile. *I'll take a nice long bubble bath and watch a movie. Maybe I'll even eat some of the Chunky Monkey ice cream Mom hid in the freezer in the garage.*

As she twisted the knob to her room, muffled noises sounded from inside. She froze, imagining for a moment an axe-wielding gruesome zombie she'd glimpsed in a movie Zayd and Fadi had been watching the other week. *Don't be a scaredy-cat.*

The door swung open, revealing Laila sitting on the bed, her eyes puffy and red.

"What's wrong?" asked Ariana, thoughts of a quiet evening going up in smoke.

"Your father got an e-mail from one of his friends from Kabul," Laila said, sniffing.

"And?" prodded Ariana.

"He didn't know I was listening, but he called Uncle Shams. He told him that even though the American military is looking for my father, there are rumors . . ."

Rumors. I hate rumors. Ariana gritted her teeth.

"Rumors that the *Taliban* kidnapped my father."

Shocked, Ariana slumped next to Laila. "How can that be?" she whispered.

"He went missing in a Taliban-controlled area," said Laila. "And since my father is considered a traitor for working for the Americans, he's on their wanted list."

Ariana's mind went into overdrive. "Have they received a ransom note?"

"Your father didn't say anything about that," said Laila. "After he hung up, he went next door with my mom, your mom, and Hava Bibi."

So that's why Uncle Shams was in such a rush to get

home, thought Ariana. She grabbed her cousin's hand. "Look, it's just a rumor. And if there's no ransom note, they most likely don't have him."

"Or . . . ," whispered Laila.

"No!" Ariana burst out. "Don't even think it. You *have* to be positive."

"I've been trying to," said Laila, her voice cracking. "But every time the phone rings, I get nervous. And the news has just been getting worse and worse."

Ariana reluctantly nodded, but as she looked around their cramped room, she felt restless. "Look, we can't just sit around here feeling sorry for ourselves."

"Yes, I can," said Laila, being uncharacteristically stubborn.

Ariana grabbed her cousin's arm and dragged her off the bed. "Come on. We're going to go find some answers."

"But, Ari, nobody ever tells us anything," wailed Laila, but she allowed herself to be led out of the room.

"Don't worry. We'll find a way, but first we're going to find something to eat," said Ariana.

Since there was no one around to tell them they couldn't, they made banana splits with the Chunky Monkey ice cream, dollops of whipped cream, chocolate syrup, and chopped pistachios. *Might as well be miserable on a full stomach.* They took their bowls and settled in front of the TV, which they were usually not allowed to do. One of Mariam's favorite reality shows, *Take That*, was on. This particular episode featured a young woman who'd gotten a terrible nose job from an unethical plastic surgeon. She'd showed up at his fancy office and was confronting him, not only to get her money back but also to take back her sense of power and to stop feeling like a victim. *Weird*, thought Ariana, changing the channel, going past a Disney movie they'd already seen. Laila listlessly poked at her sundae, not really paying attention. She kept turning her head toward the front door, waiting for the adults to come home; only they knew what was happening with her father. Over the blare of the TV, they finally heard the front door open an hour later, and the girls sat up in anticipation.

"Hey," shouted Baz, "one of my buddies lent me Goblin Invasion."

"No way I'm playing that," complained Hasan. "That's so boring. I have Arctic Hunt and Super Mario. Let's play one of those instead."

"Hey," interrupted Omar. "Mom said no playing anything till our homework's done.

"Aw, man," complained Hasan. "We can do it after playing."

"Yeah, *you* tell her that," Omar shot back.

Darn, thought Ariana. They'd been invaded by the boys. "Come on," she told Laila, pulling an evasive maneuver. "We have a lot of work to do before tomorrow night."

"What's tomorrow night?" asked Laila, blinking in confusion.

Ariana gave her a playful punch on the arm. "It's only the *best* night of the year! *Halloween.* We dress up and go trick-or-treating."

"Oh, right," said Laila, perking up a little. She'd been amazed when they'd explained to her how you went to people's houses and they gave you free candy.

Before they could slip into the garage, they ran smack into the boys in the hall. Spotting Laila, they instantly quieted and gathered around, their eyes downcast.

"Hey, guys," said Omar.

"We heard the rumors about your dad," said Hasan, his voice low. "I'm really sorry."

"Yeah," added Omar as Marjan leaned over and hugged her.

Little Taroon, feeling left out, snuggled into Ariana.

Taken aback, she squeezed him with one arm and kissed the top of his head. He smelled like strawberry shampoo and popcorn.

"We all prayed that he'll be found soon," said Baz, his freckles bright against his pale face.

"Thank you so much," said Laila, looking away to stop herself from crying.

Sensing tears about to erupt, the boys dispersed like ghosts, and the girls entered the garage to inspect their costumes. Every year Ariana and Mariam made their costumes themselves. Last year they'd gone as salt and pepper shakers, and the year before they'd been Little Bo Peep and one of her sheep. This year Laila was joining them, so they'd decided to be different-colored M&M's. Mariam, of course, was going to be pink, even though it wasn't a standard color. The boys were going to be one superhero or another, again, which was easy. They recycled the Superman, Spider-Man, and Hulk costumes amongst themselves. Zayd thought Halloween was childish, so he and Fadi were hanging out at home, watching a movie.

"Come on," said Ariana, grabbing the two huge circles of blue and green felt. Hava Bibi had sewn two rounds together, then turned them inside out to hide the seams. Luckily, the seams weren't touching Ariana's skin, so she was okay with that. She'd just wear one of her supercomfy T-shirts and sweatpants underneath. Their grandmother had left open sections on the top and bottom for their head and legs. Two small holes on the sides were for their arms. Now all they had to do was cut out an *M* from white felt and glue it on.

While they waited for the glue to dry, Laila found a cozy spot next to the desk and cracked open a book they were reading in language arts, *Shaka, King of the Zulus*. Ariana debated reading but decided to sort through her origami supplies instead. As she went to pick up her box, she noticed a bag of colorful scraps of paper, probably from her father. Usually if he came across interesting paper, he saved it for her. She dumped out the bag and started sorting. Most of it she'd throw away, but she found a nice piece of metallic paper that felt rough and crinkly, and a silky square of leftover wrapping paper. At the bottom of the pile she came across a couple of familiar faces— Ana Cardoso's and Ronald Hammersmith's campaign flyers from the fall festival.

Ronald's flyer, made of heavyweight and slightly textured stock, felt pleasantly solid in her hand. She remembered that she needed a green shade of paper like this to make the trees for her zoo menagerie, so she took it over to the desk. When the page caught the light of the lamp, its blue-green hue brightened, and as her fingertips slid across the page, it somehow felt familiar. With a slight frown she reached for her magnifying glass and looked more closely. Her breath caught in her throat; tiny smudges peppered the page. She opened her father's filing cabinet and yanked out the folder of clues she'd hidden in the back. She removed the sunflower-yellow horse meat flyer and laid it beside Ronald's flyer. In comparing the two she noted that the paper quality was the same—expensive, manufactured of cotton pulp that, when torn, frayed ever so slightly.

"Laila," she whispered, her tone urgent. "Look at this."

14

Kami Clues

AFTER SCHOOL THE NEXT day Wali, Ariana, and Mariam biked over to Krishna Kopymat, a few blocks away from Wong Plaza. The night before, Ariana had sent Wali and Mariam an e-mail as soon as she and Laila had stopped puzzling over the two flyers. Today Laila had gone home to cover for Ariana with her parents and Hava Bibi. If they asked, her cousin was to tell them that she'd gone over to Mariam's to drop off some schoolbooks. The trio locked up their rides and pulled off their helmets.

"Show us," said Mariam with an eager smile as she and Wali crowded around.

"Look," said Ariana, holding up the two pages. "This is the same type of paper—heavyweight, a bit textured. And notice how they both fray at the edges? The ink smudges on both of them too."

"Wow," murmured Wali, rubbing the paper between his fingers. He glanced up at Ariana with newfound respect. "It's amazing how you could know all that from just looking at them. To me all paper looks the same."

Ariana blushed at the unexpected compliment. "I just know a lot about paper," she managed to mumble.

Mariam grinned. "All those years of origami paid off."

The bell at the top of the door clanged as they entered Krishna's, startling the skinny young clerk who was stacking boxes at the other side of the store.

"How can I help you?" he asked. His nametag read Raj K.

"Hi," said Wali. "We need your help with these."

Ariana laid both flyers on the counter. "We think they were printed by the same print shop. Was it here?"

Raj examined the sheets, holding them up to the light, feeling the texture and examining the torn edges. "Well. Although the color is different, this is definitely the same brand of paper."

Ariana released a pent-up sigh. *I was right!*

"How can you be so sure?" asked Mariam.

"When I just looked at it through the light, I saw that both have the same thickness and transparency, which allows a sheet of paper to conceal print on the opposite side. And they have the same grain direction, since paper, like wood, has a grain."

"What's that?" asked Ariana, fascinated.

"Grain is created in the paper-making process," said Raj, warming up before his audience. "The fibers of the raw pulp are poured over a continuously moving fine mesh belt. The water is drained and pressed out of the pulp, and the moving belt causes the fibers to line up in the direction of the motion. Paper can have either a short or long grain, and both of these have a long grain. They also have the same slightly rough texture and matte finish."

"Wow," muttered Wali.

"Yeah. Well, my dad is pretty serious about this stuff since it's our business," said Raj with a hint of pride.

"So do you have this type of paper?"

"Nah, we don't carry recycled paper."

"Recycled?" said Ariana.

"Yeah," said Raj. He held up the page and showed a small watermark in the bottom corner—the symbol

for recycling. Three mutually chasing arrows form-
ing a Möbius strip. Ariana hadn't thought to hold the
paper up to light, so she'd missed the marks. "This
ink is also unique," added Raj, smelling both pages.
He held it out to them to sniff. "Notice how it doesn't
smell harsh, like chemicals?"

The others nodded. It smelled a little waxy.

"That's because it's not a regular ink," said Raj. He
put it down and rubbed the front with his thumb.

"It smudges a bit," said Ariana.

"Because its soy ink," said Raj.

"Soy like soybeans?" asked Mariam.

"Yup. Soy ink is made from soybeans and is environmentally friendly, unlike traditional petroleum-based
ink. And the clincher is that it doesn't smell like harsh
chemicals. Some say soy-based inks provide more
accurate colors. It does make it easier to recycle the
paper it's printed on, but soy ink is also slower to dry,
so we don't use it."

"Oh," said Ariana, deflated. "So you *definitely* didn't
print these?"

"No, these aren't ours, though they're beautifully
made."

"Do you know who could have printed them?"
asked Wali.

"I'd suggest a green, ecological printer," said Raj. "Check the yellow pages. There are a few in the area."

"Thanks for your help," said Mariam.

"No problem," said Raj.

The trio tumbled out of the store, energized by their first real clue.

"That was awesome," said Wali. "He knew so much about paper. Who knew there could be so many kinds?"

"Too bad the flyers aren't from his store," said Ariana.

"I know," said Mariam, staring at both the flyers clutched in her hand. "But he provided us with a really important clue."

"What clue?" grumbled Ariana, desperate to find answers.

"He showed us that Ronald's leaflet and the horse meat flyer were printed up by the same store," said Mariam.

"That's right," said Wali. "We just need to find that store."

"We need to find the store fast," said Ariana, thinking back to Uncle Shams and his anger toward the Ghilzais. "I'm worried that something else is going to happen—something bad."

"I'm worried too," said Wali as Mariam nodded.

"Okay, Mariam. Can you dig up a list of green printers?" asked Ariana.

"Sure, no problem," replied Mariam.

"Wali and I still need to follow up on the last couple of suspects on our list—Mr. Hooper, who's retired, and Fiona."

"Didn't Mr. Martinez say Fiona was in the hospital the night of the break-in?" asked Wali.

"I know, but we can't cross her off till we know for sure," said Ariana.

"Okay," said Mariam. "Let's do it." With that the trio headed home, the weight of their tasks heavy on their shoulders.

Ariana paused at the front door, inhaling the crisp autumn air. It smelled faintly of wet grass and ash from cozy fires.

"Have a ghoulishly fun time, girls," Jamil said. He was wearing a jester's hat and was loading up the candy bowl.

"Thanks, Dad. We will," replied Ariana. She paused a moment as the other two girls said their good-byes and headed outside for a much anticipated night of trick-or-treating.

"Dad," said Ariana. "Whatever happened to that

woman, Leslie something or other, the one who wanted to rent Kabul Corner to turn it into a pizza parlor?"

"Oh, she was just scoping out locations," said Jamil, dumping out the bag of mini chocolate bars.

"So she didn't call again?" prodded Ariana.

Her father gave her an odd look. "No. I sent her to Lucinda, since I knew John Hooper wanted to cancel his lease after his heart attack. The diner already had a kitchen, so it would have been perfect for her. But I guess she never followed up."

"Oh," said Ariana, mentally checking Leslie off the list. If she'd been serious about the pizza joint, she could have converted Hooper's Diner.

"Why do you ask, *jaan*?" asked Jamil, his jester bells ringing.

"It's nothing," said Ariana, hurrying out the door. "Just curious."

Jamil shrugged and picked up another bag of candy.

The sun had set half an hour before, setting the scene for a spooky night. The girls headed out in the opposite direction from the boys, who were being chaperoned by Sara *Khala*. Even Laila had a carefree smile as she clutched her pillowcase, anticipating the night's haul. Her eyes wide, she looked down the street, admiring the jack-o'-lanterns sitting on windowsills, the flying witches, cobwebs, and other decorations adorning the houses. There had been no news from Afghanistan, which in a way was a good thing, as they kept praying that Uncle Hamza would be found soon, safe and sound.

"So, what did you find out about green printers?" asked Ariana, taking the lead down the sidewalk toward the Huntington house, where they gave out full-size Twix bars.

"There are eleven printers that do some kind of environmentally friendly printing, all within a fifteen-mile radius of the city," said Mariam.

"That's a lot," muttered Ariana. "Is there any way to narrow them down?"

"I called one of them, and they said that they'd have to see the flyer in order to see if it was their print job or not."

"That could take forever," said Ariana, ready to ring the Huntingtons' doorbell.

After depositing the candy in their bags, they plodded on.

"The Krishna Kopymat guy said that the flyers came from the same place, right?" asked Laila.

Mariam and Ariana nodded. Ariana had filled her cousin in on all that they had learned from Raj.

"Well, you know one of the customers already," said Laila.

A grin spread across Ariana's face. "Ronald Hammersmith!"

"Well, why don't you just ask him where he had it printed?" asked Laila.

"That's a brilliant idea," exclaimed Mariam, patting Laila on the back.

Ariana laughed, giving Laila a hug. "I'll call his office tomorrow."

As they rejoiced by sharing a box of Milk Duds, the familiar, sharp wail of a fire truck siren echoed up the main road, parallel to them. Ariana's ears perked up. It was accompanied by the wail of a police car.

"I hope no one's hurt," said Mariam, stopping at the next house.

Laila looked in the direction the sirens were heading and pointed up to the sky. Ariana saw silvery smoke billowing up, veiling the bright white moon. A hard knot developed in her stomach; the Milk Duds suddenly were making her nauseous. She had a terrible feeling about the fire.

15

Fire Proof

"SOMEBODY, GET THE DOOR!" hollered Nasreen as
the bell rang the next afternoon.

With none of her brothers in sight or earshot,
Ariana trudged over to see who it was. As the door
swung open, she froze. It was Officer Nguyen and
his partner standing on the front step. As she took
in his friendly, tanned face, the line he'd written in
the police report flashed in her mind. *We found no
sign of forcible entry into the store.* For a brief second
she was tempted to blurt out that a mysterious third
party might be behind the horse meat flyers and the
break-in at Kabul Corner. But she kept her mouth

shut. Officer Nguyen would most probably think she had an overactive imagination, especially since there was no real proof to support the claim.

"Hello," she croaked, taking a steadying breath.

"Hi there. Is Jamil Shinwari home?" asked Officer Nguyen.

"Uh, yeah," said Ariana. "I'll go get him." She raced to the kitchen, where her father was reading the newspaper over a cup of tea and uneaten toast.

"Dad, Officer Nguyen is at the door with his partner. He wants to talk to you." Jamil practically jumped from his seat, his body tense as he rushed to the door. Ariana followed him back, noticing that he looked thinner; all the stress of the past few months was taking a terrible toll on his health and he was barely eating or sleeping.

"Good morning, Officer Nguyen," said Jamil. "Is there another problem at Kabul Corner?"

"No, nothing happened at your store."

"Thank goodness," said Jamil, his smile strained.

"But we're here because of another incident at Wong Plaza," explained Officer Nguyen. "There was a fire at another store there last night."

"Oh, no," said Jamil, gripping the door, his knuckles white.

"Unfortunately, the damage to Pamir Market was severe," he added, pulling out his notebook.

"Pamir Market?" Jamil repeated, the color draining from his face.

What? thought Ariana. *How could this have happened?* Then she remembered the wail of the fire trucks passing by the night before.

"It looks like an accident," said Officer Nguyen.

"An accident?" repeated Jamil, as if not quite believing the news.

"Yes, one of the ovens in the bakery short-circuited, causing an electrical fire."

An oven caught on fire? thought Ariana. *That sounds way too convenient.* "There was no sign of a break-in?" she blurted out before she could stop herself.

Her father and Officer Nguyen both gave her an odd look. "Actually, no. There was no sign of forced entry. Both the front and back doors were locked when the fire department arrived."

"Oh," muttered Ariana, and she ducked away into the living room, still within earshot of what they were saying. *There was no forced entry, like at Kabul Corner!*

"We're asking all the tenants a few questions."

"Of course," said Jamil.

"Can you tell us where you were last evening, between six and eight o'clock?"

"I was home," said Jamil, "handing out candy to trick-or-treaters. My wife and mother were home with me."

Ten minutes later the police were gone and Jamil left for the store. Ariana paced the kitchen, not fully comprehending what had happened. Laila sat at the table, a forgotten bowl of soggy cornflakes in front of her.

"I looked for Wali at school all day and now I know why he wasn't there," exclaimed Ariana. "I bet his father is going to blame the fire on Father. I just know it."

Laila nodded. "Call him. Find out what's going on at his house."

Ariana dialed Wali's number with shaking fingers, hoping his father wouldn't pick up. A feminine voice answered the phone.

"Hi, um . . . this is Wali's friend from school. Is he home?" Ariana asked.

"Just a sec," the voice replied.

"Hello?" said Wali.

"Wali, it's Ari," she said breathlessly.

"Hold on," he whispered. "I've got to find a quiet

place to talk." There was a rustling noise and the click of a door closing.

"I'm so sorry about your store," Ariana burst out. "A police officer just came to our house and told us about the fire."

There was a pause at the other end of the line, and Ariana's heart pounded at twice the speed. *Does he think my father or Uncle Shams did it?* "My father didn't have anything to do with it," she said, close to tears. "I swear—he was at home giving candy out to the trick-or-treaters. My uncle was at his house too."

"I believe you," Wali finally whispered. "But my dad is beyond angry. All the money he put into the store is gone. He wants *badal.*"

Ariana sank to the kitchen floor, clutching the phone to her ear. She glanced at Laila, who mouthed *Ronald Hammersmith* to her. Ariana nodded. "Hang in there, Wali. I'm going to call Ronald Hammersmith's office and find out the name of his printer," she said. "Maybe that will get us closer to whoever is behind all of this. I'll call you right back."

"Okay," said Wali. "I'll be here."

Ariana ran into the garage, followed by Laila. Inside the file of clues lay Ronald's campaign flyer with his website address. Within seconds Ronald's smile filled the screen. He sat beside his wife and two sons, posing next to a vibrant rose garden blooming beside a sprawling mansion. The white stucco and red tile roof reminded Ariana of the house they would never own, and she felt a twinge of sadness. The other night she'd been tempted to ask her dad if he'd forfeited the deposit, but hadn't had the guts to do it. *Stop feeling sorry for yourself. We have a mystery to solve before it's too late.* On the right side of the screen was a button labeled CONTACT US. She clicked through and found the address for his campaign headquarters, which was located at his office building, along with his e-mail address and phone number.

A breathless woman picked up the phone after a few rings. "Ronald Hammersmith for mayor, campaign headquarters. How can I help you?"

"Hi," said Ariana. "I'm a big supporter of Mr. Hammersmith and need some information about his campaign."

Laila gave her a thumbs-up.

"Oh, is this the press?" asked the woman. "Ronald is happy to make time for an interview, though elections are four days away."

That's right, thought Ariana. Elections were the first Tuesday in November.

"No, no, I'm not from the press," said Ariana hastily.

There was a momentary silence at the other end. "Oh, then what can I help you with?" asked the woman, sounding less interested.

"You see," said Ariana, "I'm a student from Brookhaven Middle School in Fremont, and I'm the president of a club called the . . . er . . . the Green Recycling Society. Our teacher told us that Mr. Hammersmith is dedicated to green practices and that he uses recycled paper for his campaign flyers."

Ariana collapsed in a chair, slapping her head. *I sound like a moron!*

Laila patted her on the shoulder. "You're doing great," she whispered.

"Recycling society?" said the woman. "Look, honey, elections are coming up and things are very busy here."

"I know. I'm *really* sorry to bother you, It's just that we wanted to know where you had your *amazing* flyers printed up."

"Is that it?" grumbled the woman.

"Uh, yes," said Ariana, her fingers crossed.

There was a pause and a long sigh. "Hold on. Let me look that up for you."

Ariana jumped up and down and gave Laila the thumbs-up.

Leaf Designs was located in downtown Fremont, on the corner of Mowry Avenue and Paseo Padre Parkway. Ariana was winded after the twenty-minute bike ride there. Wali was waiting by his bike, helmet in hand.

"Before we go in, I have something to tell you," said Ariana, huffing from the long ride. "Something Officer Nguyen mentioned when he was at our house."

"Okay," said Wali. He looked terrible. His usually smooth hair was in tangles, and he had circles under his eyes as if he hadn't slept for days.

"He said that both the doors at Pamir Market were locked when the fire department got there."

"Yeah, I know," said Wali. "The fire marshal explained that to my dad, and that's why he doesn't know whether to be mad at you guys or not. There's no proof someone broke in and started the fire. Supposedly one of the ovens shorted, causing a spark."

"I know, but then Officer Nguyen used the same words he'd written in the break-in report for Kabul Corner. He said there was *no sign of forced entry*."

"But why is that so strange?" asked Wali, rubbing his eyes as if his head hurt. "Only my dad and Tofan

Baba have keys to the store, and they locked up before they left. No one else could have gotten in without a key, or locked up after."

"Well, what if someone wanted to make it look like an accident?" pondered Ariana, pacing next to their bikes. "Whoever got into Kabul Corner didn't have a key either—only my dad and Uncle Shams did. Maybe someone got into Pamir Market the same way, without using force, set the fire, and locked the doors behind them when they came out, covering their tracks."

"But who would go to so much trouble?" said Wali.

"That's what we need to find out," said Ariana, her fist clenched.

Wali paused a moment as he opened the door for her. "You know, we wouldn't have gotten this far if it weren't for you," he murmured.

"It's just that I . . . well, I pay attention to details," said Ariana, her cheeks reddening.

"Yeah, well, we're darn lucky that you do," he said, allowing her to pass through.

With the two flyers safely in a folder, she practically ran into the brightly lit store, which thankfully didn't have too long a line at the counter.

"Hi. My name is Melody. How can I help you

today?" asked the petite clerk with long, frizzy brown hair. Her bright green shirt had a leaf stenciled on the pocket.

Ariana pulled out Ronald's campaign flyer and placed it on the counter. "Mr. Hammersmith's staff mentioned that they had these printed here."

"Oh, yeah," she said with a white toothy smile. "We designed and printed these up for them. They spared no expense, only wanted the best. They have a lot of their printing done here. They say we're the best in town."

"It's really very nice," said Wali, causing the girl to smile wider.

Ariana pulled out the bright yellow horse meat flyer and placed it beside the other one. "Was this printed here too?"

Melody frowned, picking up the flyer. "We didn't design this," she said, causing Ariana's heart to plummet. "But yes, we did print them."

Wali and Ariana exchanged a triumphant look.

"Who was it?" they asked in unison.

"Huh?" asked Melody.

"We mean, who placed the order?" asked Wali, his excitement coursing toward Ariana like an electric current.

Melody frowned. "Well, it's against our company policy to share customer information."

Disappointment left a bitter taste in Ariana's mouth. *We've come so close to finding out!*

"Look," said Wali, giving her his most charming smile. "I realize you don't want to break any rules or anything, but this is really important. Mr. Hammersmith wouldn't have sent us to you if it weren't."

Ariana blinked at the white lie, and caught on to what Wali was trying to do. Ronald hadn't *exactly* sent them *personally*; his secretary had just given them their printer's name. But the fib seemed to have gotten Melody's attention, and she stared at the flyer, biting her lower lip.

"Ronald said you would totally help us out," Ariana jumped in.

"Oh," said Melody, looking a little confused as Ariana apologized to God for yet another white lie.

"Yup, that's what he said," emphasized Wali.

"Okay. It's a little odd he'd say that, but I guess I can tell you who it is, since you already kind of know," said Melody.

Ariana shared a confused look with Wali, who asked, "We already know?"

"Well, yeah," said Melody. "It was his assistant."

"Whose assistant?" asked Ariana, perplexed.

Melody's friendly smile faded as she stared at them with uncertainty in her eyes.

"Oh, *that* assistant," said Wali with a fake laugh. "There are *so* many of them."

Ariana looked at Wali like he'd lost his marbles.

Melody shrugged. "Yeah, I know. Mr. Hammersmith has a lot of people who work for him. They're always coming in and out of here, but I'm talking about Paige, the tall girl with the long blond hair."

Ariana stood tongue-tied, not quite believing what she'd heard, but Wali kept his cool. "So you're sure it's Paige, the one from his campaign staff?"

"Uh-huh," said Melody. "I remember her because she's so nice and recommended her hair stylist to me."

Ariana and Wali stared at each other, stunned. Someone named Paige in Ronald's office had printed up the horse meat flyers. They now knew *who* had printed up the flyers, but now they needed to find out *why*.

16

Changing Fortunes

WHEN ARIANA GOT HOME, the entire house was in chaos, crammed with people running around, sitting, standing, talking, shouting, and weeping. Her heart lodged in her throat, Ariana's first thought was that something terrible had happened. As she held her backpack in a death grip, she noticed that even though Sara *Khala* had tears rolling down her plump cheeks, she was also laughing. Next to her, Hava Bibi gave a great whooping laugh and hugged Zainab *Khala*, who dabbed her eyes with a tissue, looking worn out.

Laila bounded over to Ariana and gave her a huge hug. "They found him," she cried, her tiny nose red.

"What?" said Ariana, still not fully processing what was happening, but she was over her initial fright.

"They found my father," said Laila, dragging her over to the sofa.

"Oh my gosh," cried Ariana, her trip to Leaf Designs momentarily forgotten. "That's amazing news!"

"He was hiding in a farmer's field," explained Laila. "He'd dug a hole under a tree and lay there for ten days."

"How did he end up there?"

"After he got separated from his unit, he left the village, since he was still in Taliban territory and wearing a uniform, so he couldn't trust anyone. First he hid in the outlying forest, but there was no food or shelter, so he found a farm, managed to steal some bread, and hid under the tree. In the end the farmer's son found him, and it turned out that the farmer was a kind man, and he helped him out."

"Is he okay?" asked Ariana, horrified at the conditions her uncle had endured.

"He's lost weight and has frostbite on his toes, but he's alive."

"C'mon, girls. We have a lot of cooking to do," said Nasreen, rolling up the sleeves of her blouse. "We've invited friends and family to come over, including Mariam. It's a celebration!"

Ariana's heart sank as she remembered that she'd told Wali that they'd meet up later that afternoon, along with Laila and Mariam. But now that was impossible. She grabbed Laila's hand and pulled her aside. "We found out who had the horse meat flyers printed up."

"Who?" Laila gasped.

"It was someone from Ronald Hammersmith's office—one of his assistants."

"WHAT?" cried Laila, her eyes widening in shock.

Ariana gripped her arm. "Shhh. . . . I know—we couldn't believe it either. Why would Ronald or his assistant want to ruin Pamir Market's reputation?"

"It makes *no* sense," whispered Laila.

"We need to make sense out of it," said Ariana. "Wali wants us to meet later."

"We can't leave right now," said Laila, eyeing her mother and Sara *Khala* planning the menu.

Ariana nodded. "I'll take care of it."

Silence greeted Ariana as she slipped into the garage. Perfect. She had privacy to call Wali and Mariam and coordinate when and where they were going to meet up. Stepping toward the desk, she spotted her calendar; a stretch of white boxes sat empty, abandoned like the house she'd never live in. Surprisingly, instead of hot, pulsating anger, she felt cold resolve. Yes, she was disappointed, hurt, and resentful, but honestly, there were bigger things in life to worry about than not having a room of her own. She ripped the calendar off the wall, crumpling Snoopy's head with a satisfying crunch just as the garage door opened. Ariana whirled around and saw her father.

"Hey, kiddo," he said, looking more relaxed than she'd seen him in weeks.

"*Salaam*, Dad," she said, taking a deep, calming breath.

"Isn't it wonderful news about Hamza?" he asked.

"Amazing," said Ariana. "It's such a relief that he's okay."

"I know. We got the call a few hours ago," said Jamil. "We all needed that, a bit of good news for a change."

Ariana looked at her father, the shadows under his eyes and the exhaustion lining his face, and nodded.

"What do you have there?" he asked, staring quizzically at her calendar.

"Uh, it's nothing," said Ariana, hiding the calendar behind her back.

Her father gave her a shrewd look. "Come here," he said softly.

As Ariana came close, he enveloped her in a huge bear hug. Warmed to the bones, Ariana inhaled his familiar scent—aftershave and a hint of cardamom from his habit of drinking green tea. "You've been a great help to me these past few weeks, Ariana *jaan*," her father whispered into her hair.

"Really?" said Ariana, thinking that he mainly thought that she got in the way all the time and was too nosy for her own good.

"With all the challenges our family has faced, you have been there, helping both at home and at the store. You've been so kind and generous with your time, especially with Laila."

"Oh," said Ariana, not realizing that he'd noticed. The calendar dropped from her fingers and she couldn't help but finally ask. "Are we going to lose the house?"

Jamil sighed and let her go. "Well, I'm not surprised, with all that's been going on, that you found out about that."

"I overheard you and mom talking," Ariana confessed. "And I know things haven't been going well at the store."

Jamil nodded. "I came very close to forfeiting the deposit, but I didn't."

Ariana's heart leapt to her throat. "What?" she mumbled.

"I was about to call and cancel the other day, but that morning we found out about the fire at Pamir Market and I forgot to do it," he explained. "Then, that evening, Haroon called."

"Haroon called you?"

"Yes." Jamil sighed. "The damage at Pamir Market is extensive and he's out of work. He wants his old job back."

"Did you hire him?"

"Shams and I talked about it for a long time. We've decided to bring him back, based on a strict contract that he's agreed to sign."

"Wow, we'll have our bread back," said Ariana, floored by the turn of events.

"It's a shame, though," said Jamil with a grimace. "Our good fortune is coming at another's expense."

Ariana nodded. With Pamir Market gone, they were back to being the only Afghan grocery store in town, with the best bread. All their old, and new, customers would come flooding back.

"So I've decided we will move ahead and get the house," said Jamil. "If things keep improving, great. If not, I can always sell the house or rent it out."

"Okay, Dad," said Ariana. Her feeling of happiness was tempered as she thought about Wali and his family. What would they do? Where would they go?

"Enjoy the garage till your room is ready. I banned the boys from this room, since I consider this to be our special space," he said, and grinned.

As she stared into his warm hazel eyes, her thoughts shifted to everything they had learned in the past twenty-four hours, and pressure in her chest built to the point where she felt like bursting. She opened her mouth, desperate to share what she and Wali had learned about the Ronald and the fake feud. *You still have no direct proof,* a little voice inside her head reminded her. She pressed her lips together and gave her dad a kiss on the cheek instead.

It took another little lie to get Ariana and Laila dropped off at the entrance of Wong Plaza the following Saturday afternoon. Ariana told her mother that Jamil had called and asked that the girls be dropped off to help out at the store. With Pamir Market now closed, Kabul Corner was overflowing with customers, so it was a believable deception. The girls stood at the curb and waved good-bye as Nasreen drove off, turning left onto Magnolia Street. Instead of walking toward Kabul Corner, they headed in the opposite direction, toward the Daily Grind Café. On the way they passed Pamir Market, or what remained of it.

"Oh, no," whispered Laila, staring at the once sleek, brand-new grocery store.

Ariana hadn't been back to Wong Plaza since the night before Halloween, and she never could have imagined the horror laid out before her. Rage blossomed deep in her bones, sending sparks of fury through her as she stared at the burned and blackened shell of Pamir Market. The wind picked up flecks of ash, which floated toward them like the tiny snowflakes she'd seen while visiting the ski slopes in Lake Tahoe the winter before. Only the *P* in "Pamir" had survived the voracious flames. The rest of the sign was gone. Beyond the boarded up windows lay inky blackness.

The roof had a hole where the fire had eaten through, then spread over the building, leaving a charred, broken skeleton of walls. The perimeter of the store was encircled by yellow police tape, warning people to stay away from the unstable structure. Traumatic memories of walking into Kabul Corner after the break-in came rushing back, flooding Ariana's mind. It was impossible to think how devastating this had to be for Wali and his family—the utter destruction of their store, and livelihood. As she averted her gaze, thinking of how Ronald or his assistant could be involved in any of this, her eyes fell on the SOLD sign on the warehouse beyond the plaza.

"Come on," said Laila, interrupting her depressed thoughts.

The light flickered green, urging them across the street toward the café. Mariam called out as the girls entered, directing them to a table tucked away in a back corner. Wali slouched in his seat, enveloped in a black hoodie, his face pale. Ariana placed the file of clues next to him, her eyes downcast.

"We just saw the store," said Laila, her voice wavering. "It's just awful."

Wali nodded, his jaw clenched. "Tofan *Baba*'s been trying to calm my father down, but he goes from being sad to really, really mad." He glanced at Ariana with dull, tired eyes. "He still thinks your father and uncle had something to do with it."

"I know." Ariana sighed. "He wants *badal*. And I don't blame him. I'd want revenge too—to get back at whoever did this."

"Ari is right," said Laila. "We have to figure out who's behind all this."

"Well, let's get to it," said Wali, pushing back his hood, his tone resolute.

While Laila opened her notepad, Ariana absentmindedly glanced toward the front door and spotted a group of men playing chess, partially hidden by a display of Thanksgiving coffee. Ariana blinked as an old memory flickered, like a movie projector whirring to life. She'd seen this exact scene before, earlier in the summer, when she'd come in to get coffee for her father and uncle. Men had been playing chess, and beside them, partially hidden by a similar display, had been Lucinda Wong, talking to a red-haired man. Ariana blinked. *Red hair.* The day at the fall festival, she'd seen Ronald Hammersmith with his ponytailed red hair and tried to remember where she'd seen him before. *It was right here.* She shook her head as if to clear it. "I know the connection between Ronald and Wong Plaza," she blurted out, her heart ramming against her rib cage.

"What?" asked Wali, sitting up, alert.

"I saw Ronald and Lucinda talking to each other here, in the café, a week before your store opened."

"You did?" asked Wali.

"So there *is* a connection between the two," cried Mariam.

"And Ronald's assistant, Paige, made the horse meat flyers," said Ariana.

"And those flyers ended up all over Wong Plaza," said Wali, opening the file of clues and dumping them out over the table.

"But why? Why would he do it?" asked Laila, looking bewildered.

"The answer must be in here somewhere," said Wali.

Mariam picked up Ronald's campaign flyer, its bold headline promising to bring "Change with Conscience." Beneath the slogan were phrases such as "environmental responsibility," "sustainable urban renewal," and "land management." "Well, he sure is worried about the environment," she said, stroking the recycled flyer. "He's into real estate, right? Since it says he's all about building green, sustainable neighborhoods."

Ariana's eyes widened. "Wali, remember the day we were at Mrs. Wong's?" Wali nodded. "The article on the front page of the *Tri City Express* was about the mayoral elections, how they were heating up. The woman running against Ronald talked about his recent land acquisitions and accused him of trying to lobby for rezoning Fremont neighborhoods. What if all these clues point to something bigger?"

"Do you really think . . . ," said Wali, his voice soft as he contemplated her words. "I mean, it kind of makes sense. He was here, talking to Mrs. Wong, the owner of a valuable piece of real estate in the middle of Fremont."

"Yup," said Ariana, fidgeting in her chair. "Ronald meets with Mrs. Wong. Then all these strange things start happening at Wong Plaza!"

"Nobody's going to believe us if we tell them about all this," exclaimed Mariam, waving her hands over the clues.

"Mariam's right," said Laila, her cheeks pink with worry. "Ronald is rich, and he's running for mayor. Nobody will believe he'd do something this awful to get his hands on a piece of property."

"They won't believe us, not until we have direct proof that it's him," said Wali, crumpling the horse meat flyer in his fist.

"Well, let's find the proof," said Ariana, feeling more hopeful than she had in a long time.

17

Truthful Digging

THE FIRST THING ON the new to-do list was to go back and visit Mrs. Wong, since it was after Ronald met with her that all the trouble began. So, while Laila headed to Kabul Corner and Mariam went home to do some research on the Internet about Ronald, Ariana and Wali made the fifteen-minute trek to Mrs. Wong's house.

It was Martin who answered the door at Ariana's insistent knock. "Hi." He smiled widely. He was wearing the same Mickey Mouse T-shirt as last time and had a Rubik's cube in his hand.

Darn, thought Ariana. *I forgot to bring him pistachios.*

"Hi, Martin," she said. "Is your mom home?"

"Yes," he said, thankfully not remembering the nuts. "I'm not allowed to let you in. I'll go get her."

The door shut, and Mrs. Wong opened it a few minutes later, looking disheveled, as if she hadn't had time to shower

"Hello, Mrs. Wong," began Ariana. "We're sorry to bother you again, but we're working on a school project and wanted to interview you."

"A school project?" asked Mrs. Wong.

"Yes," said Wali. "It's for social studies, a project on civics and government."

"Oh," said Mrs. Wong, glancing at her watch. "I can talk to you for a few minutes, but it'll have to be fast, since I need to get ready and leave for church in fifteen minutes."

"Sure, no problem," said Ariana as she followed Wali inside.

"How is your father doing, Wali?" asked Mrs. Wong.

Wali grimaced. "He's okay, considering what happened. He called the insurance company, and the adjustor is coming on Tuesday to give damage estimates."

"I talked to your father last night. He's very upset, as am I," said Mrs. Wong, dabbing her eyes with her sleeve.

Ariana realized Mrs. Wong was hiding tears, and

Ariana swallowed back anger. *How could anyone torment a nice woman like Mrs. Wong?* "It's really awful how terrible things keep happening," Ariana said in a soft voice.

"I know." Mrs. Wong sighed. "I just don't know what to make of it. Ever since the summer ended, we've been plagued with such bad luck. Who would think a brand-new oven would short out?" *Short out, my foot,* thought Ariana. "But thank the Lord that the fire didn't spread to the other stores."

"The fire department showed up right on time," said Wali.

Mrs. Wong nodded, and then brought the conversation back to why they were there. "So, how can I help you two today?"

Ariana and Wali had decided not to tell her about their investigation or share their suspicions. They had worked out a cover story and were sticking to it.

Wali cleared his throat. "As I mentioned, we're working on a project for social studies and have chosen to study the election process—in particular, the mayoral race."

"Oh, that sounds interesting," said Mrs. Wong, perking up.

"Yes, it is," Ariana said, cringing at the fib as she

flipped open her notebook. "We're researching all the candidates for mayor, including Ronald Hammersmith."

"We wanted to get your thoughts, since you know him," Wali slipped in.

"Oh," said Mrs. Wong with a frown. "I don't actually know him that well."

"But you were talking to him at the Daily Grind Café a few months ago," Ariana prodded, looking down at the page, pretending to take notes.

Mrs. Wong shrugged. "Well, we met because he wanted my support for his candidacy, so I gave him a small donation and endorsed him."

Ariana's stomach sank. *Is that it?*

"Why did you endorse him?" asked Wali.

"I strongly believe in environmental protection and sustainable development," said Mrs. Wong, "which is a large part of his platform."

"Yes, that's what we've found out about him too," said Wali, pulling out Ronald's campaign flyer. "These are printed on recycled paper."

Ariana thought back to what she'd read in the *Tri City Express,* and the words came tumbling out of her mouth. "Ronald has been buying up land for green development projects."

"It's funny you say that," said Mrs. Wong, folding

her hands in her lap. "As our meeting was ending, Ronald surprised me by mentioning an interest in buying Wong Plaza."

Ariana stared at Mrs. Wong, momentarily dumbstruck. *Buying Wong Plaza?*

Thankfully Wali wasn't as tongue-tied. "Mr. Hammersmith wanted to buy Wong Plaza?"

"Yes, but I told him I wasn't interested in selling."

"Why not?" croaked Ariana, her tongue finally loosening.

"Well, over the years many developers have wanted to buy the plaza, since it's in such a central location, between industrial and residential neighborhoods. But the land has been in my family for three generations, and I have a personal connection to it."

"Oh," said Ariana. "I didn't know that."

"Yes, but he was very persistent," said Mrs. Wong, looking a little put off at the memory. "In fact, he came by here a few weeks after we'd met and tried to sweet-talk me into selling. But I politely declined since the property is my only source of income."

"Oh, wow," murmured Ariana, sharing a triumphant look with Wali.

Mrs. Wong glanced down at her watch. "Okay, guys. We need to wrap it up soon."

"Thanks for your time, Mrs. Wong," said Wali.

"Not a problem," said Mrs. Wong as she stood up to see them out. "Although sometimes I wonder if I should just go ahead and sell, since it's becoming tough to manage all these problems in my old age."

Ariana shared a worried glance with Wali, and she knew he was thinking the same thing. *That's exactly what Ronald wants.* As they walked past the dining room, she spotted the corkboard and the line of master keys and recalled their first visit. *The keys!*

She stumbled against Wali, who steadied her. "You okay?"

She grinned. "Yup." As soon as Mrs. Wong had shut the door behind them, she lowered her voice. "I know how they got in!"

"Huh?" said Wali, a quizzical look on his face.

"Last time we were here, I told you that the master keys to our stores had been switched around—as if someone had put them back in a hurry and hadn't checked which was which. Ronald must have gotten copies of the keys somehow!"

Wali let loose a loud whoop and gave Ariana a hug. Shocked, they clonked heads and jumped back from each other, red-faced.

. . .

The next thing on their to-do list had been Mariam's idea—based on her favorite reality show, *Take That.* It was a pretty gutsy strategy, one that was going to take a lot of nerve to pull off. But if they succeeded, it would give them the evidence they badly needed. The plan was to be put in motion as soon as school ended the following Monday afternoon.

In nervous anticipation, Ariana floated in a daze, from one class to another, and at one point Mr. Lambert asked if she was sick and needed to go see the nurse. She mumbled that she was okay, but turned beet red as everyone stared at her. Hidden behind her science textbook, she'd been reading a copy of the *Tri City Express* that Wali had handed her in homeroom that morning. The news about Pamir Market was just hitting the papers, and the front page revealed a picture of the burned-out shell of the store, followed by a brief article.

Dressed in the most professional clothes they could find, Ariana and Wali arrived at Ronald's flashy glass and chrome office promptly at three fifteen. They paused in the parking lot, staring up at the shiny sign for New Vistas Development Corporation. Mariam had convinced her older brother, Fadi, to drop them off. He and Mariam would return to pick the duo up at four thirty, which would give them ample time for their operation. As Wali adjusted his too-long sports jacket, Ariana tugged at the itchy, too-small woolen pants she'd borrowed from Mariam. The matching navy cotton tunic had actually given her a rash, and she wished she could tear it off and pull on her comforting sweats. But she gritted her teeth. *If I have to suffer to gain the truth, I will.* After pushing past the heavy glass doors, they stepped into the sleek lobby buzzing with activity, and approached a harried receptionist sitting at the front desk.

"Remember," whispered Wali. "We're doing an article for the school newspaper on local elections and Ronald Hammersmith."

Ariana nodded, clutching her backpack while mentally reviewing the plan. A variety of emotions swirled through her mind. One minute she thought that the scheme was brilliant. The next she felt that it was the dumbest idea ever. *But,* she thought, and sighed, *it's the only option we have. There is no plan B.*

Wali approached the receptionist with confidence. "We're here to see Mr. Hammersmith," he said.

"Take a seat," said the receptionist, her gray eyes magnified behind large horn-rimmed glasses. "I'll be with you in a minute."

The duo took a seat on the white couch adjacent to a long oil painting of hills blooming with bright golden poppies. At the other end of the sofa sat a bearded man in a frayed tweed coat, taking notes on his laptop. Ariana ran her hand along the buttery-soft leather, rubbing it with her thumb, taking deep calming breaths.

Wali stole a glance at his binder. Inside he carried an official-looking letter from Patty, of all people. Wali and Ariana had cornered her at lunch and asked for her help. Ms. Popularity had batted her eyelashes at Wali and given Ariana a hostile look, but after hearing their story, her mouth had hung wide open. Sensing a hot story for *The Owl*, she'd agreed to do what she could to help. She'd snuck into the art studio, which served as *The Owl*'s office, and printed out a letter using the school's stationery, pretending to be Coach Newsom, *The Owl*'s adviser. The letter confirmed that two students would be visiting Mr. Hammersmith to conduct an interview for the school newspaper, which had been arranged by Principal Chiu.

"Terry Yurkovich, *Tri City Express*," called out the receptionist.

"That's me," said the man, picking up his leather

attaché case and hurrying to a set of doors leading into the main building.

A few minutes later the receptionist waved them over. "Do you have an appointment?" she asked, her tone brusque.

"Yes. Our principal, Mrs. Chiu, made it a month ago," said Wali.

"Your names?" she asked.

"Jose Rivera and Nooria Afridi," said Wali, the names rolling off his tongue as if they were the truth. "We're from *The Owl,* our school newspaper."

The receptionist looked on her computer. "I don't see your names in here."

Ariana and Wali had been expecting this, so they kicked the plan into action.

"How can that be?" said Wali loudly, looking stricken. He handed the receptionist Coach Newsom's phony letter. "Our principal sent this, confirming our visit."

Wow, he's as good an actor as Mariam, thought Ariana, impressed.

"I understand, but you don't have an appointment," said the receptionist. "We can reschedule if you'd like."

"You don't understand," Wali practically cried.

"We're doing a huge article on the candidates, and our grade is depending on us meeting Mr. Hammersmith—"

"We're going to fail," interrupted Ariana with a loud wail, and she crumpled to the floor. For good measure she started to moan, sniffing loudly.

The receptionist's eyes widened, and she looked uneasily around the lobby; everyone was staring at them, some shaking their heads in dismay.

"Hold on," said the woman, punching speed dial as Ariana started to sob loudly, holding a napkin she'd found crumpled in her pants pocket. "Can you come out here?" she hissed into the mouthpiece. "We have a situation. . . ."

A few moments later a willowy blond woman sailed through the side doors.

Ariana stiffened, recognizing her from the fall festival. She resembled the woman that Melody, from Leaf Designs, had described.

"Hey, guys," she said brightly, her white teeth flashing a strained smile. "My name is Paige Jensen, and I'm Mr. Hammersmith's assistant. What can I help you with today?"

Ariana and Wali shared a quick look. *Bingo!*

"Hi," said Ariana, her face flushed, the words

tumbling from her lips. "We're here from our school newspaper, *The Owl*, to interview Mr. Hammersmith."

"Our principal, Mrs. Chiu, made our appointment weeks ago, since we're covering local elections," added Wali. "We've already interviewed Ana Cardoso, Mr. Hammersmith's opponent."

"She was *super*nice," added Ariana, warming up. "We talked to her for *more than* an hour."

Paige bit her lip, then spoke. "I'm afraid Mr. Hammersmith is caught up in a meeting right now, but I can give you a tour till he can meet up later."

Ariana and Wali eagerly agreed, so Paige guided them through the doors Terry Yurkovich had disappeared through earlier. They stood at the entrance to a large, open work space. "This is the nerve center of Ronald's campaign," said Paige. "All these people are hard at work, since the election is less than twenty-four hours away."

The cavernous room resembled a beehive, humming with activity. Tired and disheveled staffers sat at desks, while others huddled in groups, wrote on whiteboards, or grabbed hurried cups of coffee. Ariana spotted a burly young man standing at the watercooler and recognized his crew cut and bulging muscles instantly. He'd been with Ronald the day of the festival too. He didn't seem to be doing much, just standing there, watching everyone.

"Who's he?" asked Ariana. "The guy by the water-cooler."

"Oh, that's just Gilbert," said Paige, hurrying on. "Follow me."

For the next fifteen minutes Paige took them around the campaign office, then led them to the elevators and the second floor.

"So, as you know, Mr. Hammersmith's vision for Fremont is to make it into a tourist destination by building sustainable, modern living and shopping districts."

"Yes, we read about that on his website," said Ariana.

"Check this out," said Paige, opening a door on the left. At the center of the expansive, windowless room sat a squat Formica table with a model of the city of Fremont. It was covered in tiny red, yellow, and blue flags.

"Wow," said Wali, leaning over to inspect the miniature buildings, roads, and cars.

"This model shows Mr. Hammersmith's projects that integrate materials and methods that promote natural resource conservation, improve energy efficiency, contribute to the health of employees and residents, and increase economic vitality," explained Paige. "The blue flags are completed projects, the yellows are under construction, and reds represent projects slated to begin in the near future."

Ariana inched along built-in cabinets and shelves, each labeled with names such as Greenacres Shopping Complex, Persimmon Commons, and Redwood Heights. Each shelf contained rolled sheets of paper the shade of soft turquoise, which Ariana recognized immediately; they were blueprints, similar to the ones she'd seen for the house the Shinwaris were going to buy.

As she touched the edge of the soft paper, they heard a voice booming outside. It was Ronald, and he sounded angry.

"Oh," said Paige, hastily rushing toward the door. "Why don't you guys check out the model while I take care of this." As she shut the door, Wali and Ariana hurried over to press their ears against the wood.

"I don't have time for this right now," came Ronald's retort to Paige's request that he see them. "That annoying reporter from the *Tri City Express* was here again, asking nosy questions."

"I know, but the kids said that their principal made

an appointment to see you weeks ago. Elections are tomorrow, and we can't just throw them out. They might make a stink, and the whole thing could end up on a blog by tomorrow, right before elections."

"You deal with them for now. I'll see if I can talk to them later," replied Ronald.

After some more hushed exchanges with Ronald, Paige was back. "Hey, kids! Well, with all the election craziness going on, Ronald needs another half hour or so. How about I get you settled in the conference room, and he'll swing by."

"Okay," said Wali, and they followed her across the hall to a wood-paneled room overlooking the parking lot.

"Have a seat," said Paige, pointing to the dozens of swivel chairs circling the shiny conference table. "Ronald should be in soon," she explained, then left, closing the door behind her.

As Ariana scratched her leg, tugging at the irritating seam digging into her thigh, Wali pulled out the digital voice recorder he'd hidden in his coat pocket.

"This is it," he whispered, making sure the recorder was ready, then put it back.

Ariana nodded, double-checking that the folder of clues was in her backpack, ready to be pulled out.

This is it. They were going to recreate an episode of *Take That.* Based on the format of the program, they would confront Ronald with their accusations and circumstantial evidence while secretly taping the session. Usually the culprit confessed or admitted to some of their misdeeds, and that's what they hoped Ronald would do today. Ariana sat slumped in the plush chair, doubts crowding against her belly button; although the plan had seemed pretty solid the day before, she sensed that it could very easily turn into a phenomenal disaster and get them into a lot of trouble. But they had to make Ronald confess to something, anything, that linked him to the incidences at Wong Plaza, so that they could tell their parents and the police. So they waited.

18

Blueprint Confessions

WHILE WALI DOODLED ON his notepad, Ariana drummed her fingers on the table, trying to ignore the fact that when she breathed in, the too-tight waistband of Mariam's pants dug into her stomach. Gritting her teeth, she glanced at her watch. 4:21. It had been practically an hour since Paige had left them in the conference room, and Mariam and Fadi would be coming to pick them up in less than ten minutes. Tired of sitting, she got up and paced the length of the room. "Do you think they forgot about us?" she asked.

"Maybe," said Wali, his eyes stormy. "But we can't give up yet. We *have* to talk to Ronald."

Ariana heard the desperation in his voice and cracked open the door. The hall was empty, but Ariana could hear the gentle hum of the computers in the other room. She nudged the door shut and moved toward the window, where the sun had begun to slip into the horizon. The cold glass felt good against her flushed face as she looked down to the street. Fewer cars filled the parking lot than when they'd arrived, and staffers were heading out—probably to go door-to-door, reminding people to vote—*for Ronald Hammersmith, of course.* As she was about to turn away, she caught a familiar flash of reddish hair exiting the front door. She squinted and saw the unmistakable ponytail. "Wali," she cried, waving him over.

Wali leapt from his chair and pressed his nose against the window just in time to see Ronald climb into a small hybrid car and pull away. "He's leaving!"

"What are we going to do now?" wailed Ariana.

"Crud," said Wali, thumping his fist on the glass. "We totally messed up."

A bitter sense of hopelessness settled over Ariana as she realized that they'd failed. *How could Paige just leave us here and let Ronald leave? Paige . . .* "Hey," she whispered, glancing at Wali. "What if we confront Paige instead?"

Wali blinked for a few seconds, weighing her words.

"She's part of all this," Ariana continued, a sense of renewed hope surging through her. "She's the one who ordered the flyers, so we can accuse her of trying to drive our stores out of business, like we'd planned to do to Ronald."

"It's worth a shot," said Wali, pushing away from the window. "But we have to hurry, or else she might take off too."

They grabbed their things and ran into the deserted hall.

"This way," whispered Wali, jogging toward the elevator. As they passed the room with the model of the city, Wali's steps faltered. "Wait," he said, and then he stopped altogether. He glanced down the hall, making sure it was clear, then opened the door and pulled Ariana inside.

"What are you doing?" she complained. "We don't have much time."

"I just realized something," he said, scurrying over to the model. He pointed to the center, a thoughtful look on his face.

Ariana stared down at the replica of Fremont, noting the main streets, Lake Elizabeth Park, the mall, and various neighborhoods. Freeway 880 bisected the city, and a stretch of blue on the left represented San Francisco Bay. There were a dozen flags dotting the city, each labeled something different—Greenacres Shopping Complex, Redwood Heights.

"There," said Wali, pointing down at Thornton Avenue. Ariana squinted to the east end of Thornton Avenue, where Wong Plaza sat. Behind the replica plaza stood a tiny red flag, labeled *Clay Terrace.* "Paige said the red flags were projects Ronald was about to begin," he added. "Isn't it interesting that there's a red flag right behind Wong Plaza?"

What's behind Wong Plaza? Ariana wracked her mind. Then a SOLD sign flashed in front of her eyes. The old auto parts warehouse. It had been on the market for years, until last month. She glanced back at the shelves she'd passed earlier. Each shelf had a label that corresponded to a flag on the model. She ran along the length of the room, past Greenacres Shopping Complex, Redwood Heights. . . . Finally she found what she was looking for, a shelf labeled *Clay Terrace.* A single plan lay there, rolled up in a tight scroll. Her heart thumping against her ribs, she grabbed it, brought it over to Wali, and unrolled it on the ground. There, in blue and black, lay the plans for a huge shopping district combined with an apartment

living community. And it was built on the land cur-
rently occupied by Wong Plaza.

"It's all here," said Wali, his eyes shining. With a
conspiratorial wink he folded up the blueprint, then
stuck it into her backpack.

Within a minute they'd made it down to the lobby
and exited the building.

"Where were you guys?" cried Mariam as Wali and
Ariana tumbled into the backseat of the old station
wagon. "You're late!"

"Sorry," said Ariana. "Things didn't go quite
according to plan."

"You didn't get Ronald's confession?" asked
Mariam, gripping the headrest.

"No." Wali grinned. "We got something better."

"Okay, guys," said Fadi, a twinkle in his hazel eyes.
"I know this is top secret and all, but I really hope you
didn't do anything illegal."

"No, no," said Ariana. "We didn't. . . . Not on
purpose anyway," she added, realizing that taking the
blueprint probably constituted theft.

Fadi frowned as he paused at a stop sign. "You
guys begged me for help, swearing that this was
a life-and-death matter. But I think you'd better

have answers for me when we get home."

Mariam leaned over and gave her brother a big kiss on the cheek. "You're the best brother anyone could ask for," she gushed.

"Yeah, yeah, whatever." Fadi blushed. He had a soft spot for Mariam, and she could get him to do what she wanted, within reason.

"We promise," said Ariana. "We have a lot to tell you."

"Fadi," Mariam ordered her older brother, "make it fast. We need to talk to Dad."

This is it, thought Ariana, butterflies doing the rumba in her midsection. *We're kicking into the next phase of the plan.*

The first thing Ariana did was call her mother and tell her they were at Mariam's house. Wali did the same, explaining that his friend's older brother would drop him off later. Then they went looking for Mariam's dad, Habib, who was sitting at the dining room table.

"*Salaam,* Dad," said Mariam, her voice bubbling with unrestrained energy.

The group stood at the doorway, watching Habib grade papers from a botany class he was teaching at California State University, East Bay.

"*Walaikum a'salaam, jaan,*" said Habib.

"We have to talk to you about something really important," said Mariam.

Habib frowned, running a hand over his thinning hair. "You guys are okay, right?"

"Yes, Uncle Habib," said Ariana. "Well, kind of."

"Who is this young man?" asked Habib, his gaze falling on Wali, who stood beside Fadi.

"*Salaam,* sir," said Wali, his head bowed. "My name is Wali. Wali Ghilzai."

The name sent a flicker of recognition through Habib's eyes. "You're Gulbadin's son?"

"Yes, sir," said Wali.

"I see," said Habib. He was best friends with Jamil and knew what was happening between the two stores. "I knew Professor Tofan briefly at Kabul University."

"Yes," said Wali, "he taught literature there."

Habib waved them over. "Why don't you guys take a seat and tell me what's going on."

Ariana pulled out the blueprint from her backpack and handed it to Wali, who spread it over the dining room table while she pulled out the folder of clues.

"Uncle Habib," she began after taking a deep, calming breath. "You know that things at Kabul Corner have not been going well, and that it all started when Pamir Market opened up."

Uncle Habib nodded. "Yes, Ariana *jaan*, I know the story."

"Well, everyone seems to think that the problems—the horse meat flyers, the break-in at our store, and now maybe even the fire at Pamir Market—are part of a feud that began between the Shinwaris and Ghilzais back in Afghanistan."

Habib nodded, looking intrigued and a little uncomfortable at her blunt words.

"But," said Ariana, "the weird thing is that my dad and Uncle Shams didn't know anything about the old feud. Hava Bibi had to tell them."

"Yes, my father didn't know about it either," said Wali. "Tofan *Baba* told us."

"So the old feud was left behind in Afghanistan. Our fathers had no interest in continuing it in America," said Ariana. "So when all the odd stuff began to happen, and it was blamed on the feud, it just didn't seem to add up."

"Yes," said Wali. "So, with Mariam's and Laila's help, we started digging and realized that someone was using the feud to drive both our stores out of business."

Uncle Habib's eyebrows shot up. "What?" he exclaimed. "Who would do such a thing? And how do you know this?"

"Well, like I said, it all began when Pamir Market opened up at the other end of the plaza," said Ariana.

"But," said Wali, holding up his hands, "my father didn't choose Wong Plaza because it was near the Shinwaris and he wanted to continue a fifty-year-old feud. It's just that it was the best site he could find near the Afghan community. I swear, he'd been looking for more than a year, coming up from Los Angeles to scout out locations."

"But then our baker, Haroon, left and went to Pamir Market," explained Ariana. "Father and Uncle Shams thought Wali's father had stolen him."

"But he didn't," said Wali. "Haroon came to us. He explained that he was frustrated at Kabul Corner, and my father thought it was too good an opportunity to pass up, opening a bakery."

"Sounds like a bunch of unfortunate coincidences, kids," said Uncle Habib.

"But then truly awful things started happening," said Ariana.

"The flyers," said Mariam, pulling the bright yellow page from the folder.

"Uncle Habib," said Ariana, "look at the Farsi part."

"This is a terrible translation," said Uncle Habib as he finished the last line a few minutes later.

"That's exactly what Laila thought," said Ariana.

"When these were posted all over Wong Plaza, my father was furious," said Wali.

"My dad and Uncle Shams would have felt the same if someone had written something like this about them. Wali's father came over to our store, and he and my dad kind of had it out, but my father swore he and Uncle Shams had nothing to do with the flyers, and they hadn't," Ariana added.

"Neither did our family," said Wali. "And the more we analyzed it, we realized that it didn't even look like it was written by a Farsi-speaking person."

Uncle Habib leaned back in his chair, a thoughtful look on his face.

"Then someone broke into our store and vandalized it," said Ariana. "But according to the police report, there had been *no forcible entry*, meaning no one had broken the door to get in. The windows had been broken from the *inside out, not outside in* too. But when Uncle Shams saw the destruction, he automatically blamed the Ghilzais, since neither he nor my dad remembered leaving a door open."

"But my father had nothing to do with it," said Wali.

"So you concluded that someone else was behind it all?" said Uncle Habib, his voice uncertain.

"Yes, Dad," said Mariam. "That's exactly what they're saying."

"So who do you think did it?" asked Uncle Habib, his voice skeptical.

"Ronald Hammersmith," they all said in unison.

"Ronald Hammersmith?" said Uncle Habib, an incredulous look on his face. "The politician? Why would he do such a thing?"

"Because he wants Wong Plaza," said Mariam.

"We went to see Lucinda Wong," said Wali. "She told us that Ronald has been pushing her to sell Wong Plaza to him."

"Yeah," said Ariana. "I saw them together at the Daily Grind a week before Pamir Market opened. Lucinda said that was the first time Ronald had asked her to sell Wong Plaza to him. Then he showed up at her office a few weeks later, but she still refused."

"And Ariana noticed something interesting," said Wali, giving her an approving nod. "Lucinda has all the master store keys on a corkboard at home. When Ariana examined the keys, she noticed that the Kabul

Corner and Pamir Market keys had been switched."

"Uh-huh," said Ariana. "As if someone had taken them down and put them back up in a rush, not noticing they were hanging them in the wrong spots."

"But, kids," said Uncle Habib, "there's a big difference between asking someone to sell a piece of property and performing illegal acts to get someone to sell."

Ariana pulled out Ronald's campaign flyer and handed it to Uncle Habib. "We know. That's why we needed proof that he was linked to the incidents at Wong Plaza."

"Dad," urged Mariam, "look at this next to the horse meat flyer."

Uncle Habib slipped on his glasses and peered down at the sheets as Wali showed him how to look at them through the lamplight and pointed out the recycled paper logo, the quality of the paper, and the ink smudges.

"We found out from Ronald's office that his campaign flyers were printed at a green printer—Leaf Designs. The girl who works there told us that the horse meat flyers were ordered by Ronald's assistant, Paige Jensen."

"Oh my goodness," said Uncle Habib, his disbelief eroding.

"Since we know that Ronald wanted Wong Plaza,

we realized that he had the flyers created to start a feud between the stores. It was the beginning of a plan to pressure Lucinda into selling."

"This is unbelievable," said Uncle Habib.

"There's more, sir," said Wali. He pointed to the blueprints. "This is Ronald's design for a new shopping and apartment complex. Part of it is built over Wong Plaza."

Ariana pointed to the building behind Wong Plaza. "This is the auto parts warehouse that now has a 'SOLD' sign on it."

"You should find out who bought it," piped in Fadi, standing at the door, intrigued.

"Hold on," said Uncle Habib, grabbing the phone. He put his finger to his lips for them to keep quiet, flipped on the speakerphone, and dialed. "Hello," he said when someone picked up.

"Kabul Corner. How can I help you?" came Uncle Shams's booming voice.

"*Salaam*, Shams. It's me, Habib."

"*Walaikum a'salaam*, Professor Habib. How can I help you?"

"Shams, I need a favor. Can you look out the window? Do you see the 'SOLD' sign on the warehouse behind the plaza?"

"Uh, yes, I do. Why?"

"Never mind that now. Can you give me the phone number for the Realtor listed on the sign?"

"Yes. It says 'Samuelson Realty,' and the number is 510-555-0922."

"Thanks so much. *Insha'*Allah, we'll have your family over for dinner soon."

"That would be lovely. No one makes a chicken kebob quite like you do."

With that they hung up. "Okay," said Uncle Habib, cracking his knuckles. "Keep your fingers crossed." He dialed the number for the Realtor, with the phone still on speaker.

"Hello. This is Samuelson Realty," replied a woman's voice.

"Hello. I'm interested in the auto parts warehouse off Thornton Avenue that you have listed."

"Let me look that up, sir," said the woman. A moment later she responded, "I'm sorry, but that property has been sold."

"Well, actually, I own the adjoining parcel of land and want to talk to the new owner to discuss some maintenance issues on the boundary fence," said Uncle Habib, winking at the kids for his white lie.

Aha, thought Ariana, feeling self-righteous. *Grown-*

ups bend the truth sometimes too, as long as it doesn't hurt anyone.

"Oh," said the woman. "Let me check my files." The group huddled around the phone, every second seeming like a year, until the woman came back on. "The new owners are listed as New Vistas Development Corporation."

"Thank you so much for your help," said Habib, and hung up.

"It's him," whispered Ariana, a mixture of relief, fear, and excitement coursing through her.

"That's Ronald's company," Wali said with a whoop, not able to hold in his excitement.

"What do we do now?" asked Ariana after everyone finished high-fiving.

"You leave that to me," said Uncle Habib, a shrewd look on his face.

19

Verdict's In

ARIANA'S STOMACH GRUMBLED AS she inhaled the aroma of chicken kebob wafting through the kitchen. She'd been so nervous that she hadn't eaten a bite all day, and now as she eyed the dishes that Mariam's mom had prepared—the eggplant and yogurt dip, *mantu* dumplings, chicken *pulao*, lamb and potato stew, salad, and homemade bread—she felt ravenous and nauseous at the same time. Praying that what they were about to do would work, she finished putting the forks on the serving tray while Mariam and Laila arranged cut melon in a crystal bowl. Ariana and Laila had come early to help Uncle Habib put his plan into action. The Ghilzais and Shinwaris were having dinner together, but neither family knew the other one was coming.

"Don't worry, Ari," whispered Fadi as he carried lemons in from the backyard to make lemonade. "It'll go okay."

Ariana nodded, not able to put words into a logical sentence. She focused on remembering Uncle Habib's instructions. The key to his plan lay in *timing*. He'd invited the Shinwari brothers over for six-thirty p.m. At seven p.m. Gulbadin would arrive with his family. Wali had made sure Tofan *Baba* knew the plan as well.

Ariana glanced at the clock. It was almost time. *Come on, Hava Bibi. We're counting on you,* she thought. The night before she had shared the plan with her grandmother and Laila after revealing the truth to Uncle Habib. A mix of emotions had crossed Hava Bibi's face when they'd told her about Ronald and what he'd done. After getting over her initial surprise, she was furious, then relieved that the feud was truly over, and that her boys and Gulbadin were not involved. Amazed and impressed that Ariana and Laila had uncovered the truth, she'd promised to help any way she could. As the clock struck 6:38, the doorbell rang, and Ariana stiffened. Fadi opened the door, and Hava Bibi herded the Shinwari clan into the Nurzais' cozy town house. Fadi quickly pulled Zayd into a corner and started whispering. Ariana saw her older brother's mouth fall open as he stared in her direction, while the women kissed each other on the cheeks and headed into the family room. The kids escaped upstairs to play, and under normal circumstances Ariana, Mariam, and Laila would have done the same, but tonight they had work to do. The trio stood by the front window, watching the street while Uncle Habib cornered the brothers.

"I was just on BBC's news site," said Uncle Habib. "They're reporting that Afghan security forces just averted a suicide attack on a military bus carrying army trainers and staff members to Kabul."

"Yes, I saw it on the television at the store," said Uncle Shams with a weary sigh. "A man wearing an explosive vest tried to climb aboard the bus."

Fadi frantically waved his phone at his father. This was the alert they were waiting for, Wali's text that the Ghilzais were five minutes away.

"Uh, Shams, Jamil," said Uncle Habib, steering the brothers toward his den. "I need your help with something. . . ."

"I'd be happy to help you too, Uncle Habib," said

Zayd, his voice oddly high-pitched. He took his father's arm and steered them along.

Ariana breathed a sigh of relief. Zayd was helping to keep her father and uncle busy in the den so they wouldn't see the Ghilzais arrive. Within minutes Uncle Habib was back at the front door, glancing at his watch just as the doorbell rang.

Ariana and Laila ducked into the dining room, just as Uncle Habib's wife and older daughter, Noor, came out to greet the new visitors.

"*Insha'*Allah, this will go well," whispered Laila.

"I really, really hope so," replied Ariana, squeezing her cousin's icy fingers.

"*Salaam alaikum,* Professor Tofan," said Habib, which was followed by greetings from various members of the Ghilzai family.

"We very much appreciate your invitation," said Gulbadin.

"It is our pleasure," said Uncle Habib.

Ariana and Laila watched the women retreat to the back of the house while the Ghilzai men disappeared into the living room. Like a tennis ball going back and forth, Uncle Habib popped back into the den.

"This is it," whispered Mariam dramatically.

A minute later Uncle Habib led Jamil and Uncle

Shams out of the den, followed by Hava Bibi, her features tense. As the grown-ups walked down the hall, Ariana and Laila tagged behind. All of a sudden the entourage halted at the arch leading into the living room.

Uncle Shams puffed up like a rooster. "What is the meaning of this?"

"What are *they* doing here?" shouted Gulbadin, who Ariana could see had jumped up from the sofa.

"Now, Gulbadin," said Tofan *Baba*, his voice soothing. "Calm down. . . ."

"What is the meaning of this?" shouted Shams, waving his arms like a windmill.

"This is outrageous!" said Gulbadin, turning red beneath his beard. "I will not be in the same room as the criminals who burned down my store!"

"We did not set fire to your store," said Jamil as Shams took a threatening step forward, until Hava Bibi grabbed his elbow and gave him a look that said, *Behave yourself.*

"Just because there was no sign of forced entry doesn't mean that you didn't start the fire," shouted Gulbadin.

Ariana's stomach did a somersault, and she felt sick. She made eye contact with Wali, who looked as queasy as she felt. *This is not going well.*

Before things got more heated, Habib jumped between the families, holding up his hands. "Brothers," he said, "please don't be upset. I didn't invite you here to cause distress. On the contrary, I want to help you." He looked at Jamil and Gulbadin with pleading eyes. "As my guests you will be treated only with respect, but you must be hospitable to one another, as my home is now neutral territory."

Shams, Jamil, and Gulbadin eyed one another warily as Ariana grabbed Laila's arm, holding her breath. Mariam had run to get the women, as Uncle Habib had instructed her to do.

Laila leaned over to whisper into Ariana's ear, "In *Pukhtunwali*, according to the code of *melmastia*, they need to put aside hostilities out of respect for their host."

Ariana nodded, waiting to see what the men would do.

Jamil exhaled a pent-up breath and shrugged. "Okay, Habib. Because you are my good friend, I will do as you ask. But what is so important that you had to trick us?"

"Yes, tell us," said Gulbadin, his glower diminishing only slightly.

Habib cracked a relieved smile just as a

confused-looking Nasreen, Sara *Khala,* Zainab *Khala* and Wali's mom arrived. "Sisters, please sit," said Habib. "I apologize to have brought you together using deception, but I have critical news to share, news that affects both your families."

The room quieted, and all eyes focused on Uncle Habib. "Over the past few months both Kabul Corner and Pamir Market have suffered acts of vandalism, and somehow it has been assumed that the Shinwari and Ghilzai families have been perpe-trating these acts against each other." Uncle Shams glowered, and Gulbadin harrumphed as Uncle Habib continued. "But I have just seen evidence that these nefarious activities have been perpetrated by someone else entirely, a third party."

"What?" multiple voices cried in unison.

"How can this be?" asked Jamil, rocking back in the recliner.

"What are you *talking* about, Habib?" asked Gulbadin.

"What do you mean, 'a third party'?" boomed Uncle Shams.

"Actually, it's not my story to tell," said Uncle Habib, turning toward the kids.

Ariana, her folder of clues in a death grip, shared

a nervous look with Wali, who had the blueprint clutched to his chest. As they stepped forward, Laila and Mariam joined them, the adults staring at them, dumbstruck.

"Why are the kids standing there?" asked Uncle Shams, still looking confused.

"Wali, what is the meaning of this?" asked his father.

"Why has my poor son been dragged into this?" added Wali's mother, causing Wali to wince in embarrassment.

"I hope you didn't get yourself into trouble, young lady," said Nasreen, eyeing Ariana.

Exasperated, Hava Bibi butted in. "Will everyone just be quiet and let the children speak?"

Tofan *Baba* waved his cane in the air. "Yes, yes, let them talk."

As the room quieted, Ariana cleared her throat and started to speak. "Well, it all started when Pamir Market opened. . . ." When she reached the point when Haroon left, Gulbadin interrupted. "We did not steal the baker!"

"We know," said Ariana. "Wali told me that he showed up at your house."

"He just showed up?" exclaimed Uncle Shams.

"Yes. I told you he came to us," said Gulbadin with a grim smile.

Tofan *Baba* waved his cane again, hushing them up.

"Then the awful flyers appeared," said Ariana.

"Then someone broke into Kabul Corner," said Wali.

"And the more we thought about it, we knew that our families weren't behind these terrible things," said Ariana.

"How could you know?" asked Jamil, leaning forward.

"Well," said Mariam, "I asked Wali to meet with us. We wanted to talk to him about our suspicions. We knew that neither you nor Uncle Shams had created the flyers in order to hurt Uncle Gulbadin. And Wali swore that Uncle Gulbadin hadn't broken into Kabul Corner. So the more we talked about it, we realized someone else had to be behind all of it."

"Why didn't you tell us, *bachay*?" asked Gulbadin.

"Dad, you had so many other things to worry about," said Wali. "And even though we had our suspicions, we had no proof."

"Yes," said Laila, her voice wavering a moment as Ariana gave her a reassuring glance. "To find proof we made a list of all the people who could benefit from the stores going out of business."

"Yes," added Mariam. "We investigated all the other store owners, and even Mrs. Wong, but they were all dead ends."

"You investigated them?" interrupted Wali's mother in a horrified voice.

"Mom." Wali sighed. "We promise, we didn't do anything illegal. We just snooped around a little. We also analyzed all the clues Ariana's been collecting."

"What kind of clues?" asked Gulbadin.

Ariana spent the next few minutes talking about the horse meat flyer and its poor Farsi translation, which Mariam and Laila passed around. Their audience listened with rapt attention as Ariana showed them Ronald's campaign flyer and told them how she'd noticed that both were printed on the same kind of paper, using identical smudgy ink.

Then Wali dropped the bombshell. "We found out from the clerk at Leaf Designs that both flyers had been printed there, and the horse meat flyers had been ordered by Paige Jensen, Ronald's assistant."

"Ronald Hammersmith?" said Uncle Shams in a choked voice. "But he's running for mayor!"

"But why would someone like him do something like this?" blurted out Sara *Khala,* her round cheeks flushed.

"Are you sure it wasn't just a coincidence?" pondered Wali's mother.

"No, my dear," said Gulbadin, looking at the flyers over Jamil's shoulder. "That's no coincidence."

Jamil looked at Gulbadin and nodded in agreement. "Definitely not a coincidence," he said. "But it's not direct proof either," he added.

"That's where Mrs. Wong came in," said Ariana with a triumphant smile.

"Yes," said Wali. "When Ariana and I visited Mrs. Wong, we learned a critical piece of information. She told us that Ronald had been after her to sell Wong Plaza to him."

"Oh my goodness," said Sara *Khala,* twisting her magenta scarf in her hands.

"Did you know this?" Jamil asked, sharing an incredulous look with Gulbadin and Shams.

"No, I had no idea," said Gulbadin.

"Now we had a direct link to Ronald and his interest in the plaza," said Laila. "He wanted to buy it, but Mrs. Wong wouldn't sell."

"We suspect that Ronald started investigating Mrs.

· · · 258 · · ·

Wong and found out she was strapped financially, and dependent on the rent coming in from the plaza. If any of the stores suffered, or closed down, she might be pushed to sell," Wali explained.

A stillness came over the room as the adults tried to take everything in.

"This all sounds very convincing, *jaan*," said Jamil. "But there's no direct link that Ronald did any of this."

"Wait, Jamil," said Uncle Habib, a twinkle in his eye. "Let the kids continue."

"Well, that's when Mariam had a brilliant idea," said Ariana.

Mariam explained the plan to collect the evidence they needed, based on the show *Take That*.

"You confronted Ronald Hammersmith?" said Uncle Shams, incredulous.

"What a terrible, dangerous idea!" exclaimed Nasreen, and Wali's mother nodded wholeheartedly.

"You children could have been arrested," cried Gulbadin.

"We actually didn't end up meeting him," said Wali, "but we got this." He spread out the blueprint on the carpet, and the grown-ups huddled around to look.

"That's Wong Plaza," murmured Jamil.

"Yes," said Uncle Habib, "and the plot of land behind it is that auto parts warehouse that was just sold."

"Hey, you called me for the Realtor's number," remembered Uncle Shams, turning to Habib.

"Yes, and I called them. Guess who the new owner is," said Uncle Habib.

"Ronald Hammersmith," said Uncle Shams in a small voice.

"Yes," said Uncle Habib. "All the clues the children dug up point to Ronald."

"I just can't believe this . . . ," said Nasreen, looking dazed.

"I also think I know why there was no sign of forced entry at either store," said Ariana, holding up Officer Nguyen's report. "We know that the Ghilzais didn't break into Kabul Corner, and the Shinwaris didn't set a fire in Pamir Market." She told them about Lucinda's corkboard of labeled keys, and how Kabul Corner's and Pamir Market's keys had been switched.

"Mrs. Wong mentioned that Ronald had come to her house to convince her to sell him Wong Plaza," said Wali. "He could have taken the keys and made a copy of them."

"It's my fault!" Uncle Shams groaned, holding his head in his hands.

"What are you talking about, Shams?" asked his wife.

"No, you don't understand," wailed Uncle Shams, popping up from his seat. "I went to that crook, Ronald, and told him that Pamir Market was opening and that we were very upset. It's as if I gave Ronald the idea to do these terrible things."

"Don't say that," said Gulbadin, who rose to awkwardly pat Shams on the shoulder. "None of us could have foreseen that Ronald was behind this. Who could have predicted that Ronald would find out about our old family feud and use it to try to destroy us?"

"I'm afraid I'm responsible for that," said Tofan *Baba,* clearing his throat in embarrassment. "My old friend opened his big mouth at Kandahar Kebob House a few months ago and shared the story of that darn goat starting the old feud. Obviously the gossip reached Ronald."

"Don't blame yourself either, Tofan *Baba,*" said Jamil. "You couldn't control what your friend said, or where the stories ended up."

"He could have found out about the feud multiple ways," said Ariana.

"Yeah," said Mariam. "Gossip about the feud spread like wildfire through the Afghans, but people outside the community knew about it as well. We overheard Mr. Martinez and the Smiths talking about it one day while we were . . . er . . . investigating."

"But once Ronald knew, the feud was the perfect story to cover up his crimes," said Wali.

"It was all to drive Wong Plaza under and force Mrs. Wong to sell," said Laila.

"This is just amazing," said Nasreen. "I can't believe you kids figured this all out."

Gulbadin looked at Wali with pride. "While we were feuding like fools, you were working hard to uncover the truth behind what was really happening."

"*Mashahallah,* Ariana *jaan*," said Uncle Shams, examining the flyers. "Who knew that all those years of folding paper would enable you to find these remarkable clues?"

Ariana grinned, her heart swelling with relief and pride.

Wali's mother sat with tears in her eyes. "We owe you children a great debt of gratitude."

Hava Bibi and Tofan *Baba* sat back and shared a pleased smile.

His body stiff, Uncle Shams turned to Gulbadin.

"Jamil and I were very sorry when we heard what happened to your store," he said, his voice serious. "And now that we know it was Hammersmith, I feel a great injustice has been done to all of us."

"It was a terrible blow," agreed Gulbadin. "But thankfully the insurance company has agreed to pay me for all the money I put into the store."

"Thank goodness for that," said Jamil.

"What do you plan to do?" asked Uncle Shams.

"I don't know," said Gulbadin, turning to Tofan *Baba*. "We have a few options—rebuild, or move to a different location."

"Whatever you decide to do, there is enough business for all of us," said Jamil with conviction.

"Thank you," said Gulbadin. "That is very generous of you to say."

"At least the silver lining in all this is that Ronald Hammersmith has brought your families together," said Uncle Habib, a twinkle in his eye.

"Oh my goodness," exclaimed Jamil, blinking at the mention of Ronald's name. "*He* might win the mayor's race."

He's right, thought Ariana with a jolt. In another hour the voting polls would close and the vote count would begin.

"There's no way we can let him become mayor," said Gulbadin.

"We need to do something," said Uncle Shams as the horror of that reality settled over the room.

"Well, we must tell the police what we've learned," said Uncle Habib.

"I'll call Officer Nguyen," said Jamil. "His number is in my cell phone." As he hurried to find a quiet spot to talk, Uncle Habib turned to everyone.

"*Alhamdulillah*, now we have something to celebrate! Let's eat."

As everyone scurried to lay the *dastarkhan* and bring out the food, Ariana turned to Wali and whispered, "We did it."

"We sure did," he said, and grinned back.

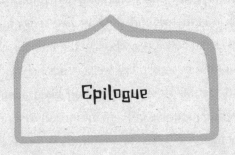

Epilogue

What's Happening

TRI CITY EXPRESS
The newspaper for the new millennium

SERVING FREMONT, HAYWARD, MILPITAS, NEWARK, SUNOL, AND UNION

"Accurate, Fair & Honest"

SCANDAL ROCKS FREMONT AS MAYORAL CANDIDATE ARRESTED ON CHARGES OF FRAUD AND ARSON

November 10, 2007

By Terry Yurkovich

FREMONT—Ronald Hammersmith, owner and president of New Vistas Development

Corporation and recent mayoral candidate, was arrested yesterday afternoon, charged with vandalism, arson, and conspiracy to commit fraud. This was the second dose of bad news for the real estate developer, who lost the race for mayor by a narrow margin last week. It has been uncovered that Mr. Hammersmith had been acquiring several properties in Fremont for redevelopment schemes, the latest of which, Clay Terrace, was financed by risky loans. Bank records reveal that Mr. Hammersmith hoped to avoid bankruptcy by rapidly building and leasing environmentally sustainable units at Clay Terrace.

"I was approached twice by Mr. Hammersmith to sell Wong Plaza, but I refused," said Lucinda Wong, owner of Wong Plaza, a critical parcel of land integral to Clay Terrace's success. Mrs. Wong's family has owned the land for three generations, and she was unwilling to part with it.

"In an attempt to force Mrs. Wong's hand into selling, Mr. Hammersmith engaged in unlawful activities," reported an unnamed source close to the Fremont Police Department. Mr. Hammersmith allegedly hired Gilbert Fargas, an ex-convict with a long record of breaking and entering.

Mr. Fargas, in collusion with another New Vistas Development Corporation employee, Paige Jensen, attempted to undermine the reputation of one of the stores at Wong Plaza, Pamir Market, by accusing them of selling horse meat masquerading as beef.

The source confirmed that Mr. Fargas confessed to entering Kabul Corner a few weeks later, with the aid of a key, which was procured by Mr. Hammersmith during a visit to Mrs. Wong's house. Mr. Hammersmith allegedly used bars of soap to make imprints of the old-fashioned master keys for Kabul Corner and Pamir Market. The locksmith who crafted the copy has been found and will be testifying at Mr. Hammersmith's trial.

Mr. Fargas also confessed that Mr. Hammersmith paid him to burn down Wong Plaza by entering Pamir Market and starting an electrical fire in one of the bakery ovens. The Fremont Fire Department reported that because of the cold, wet weather conditions on October 31, they were able to contain the fire before it spread to neighboring stores. Mr. Hammersmith has been taken into custody and is being held without bail.

· · ·

A huge grin on her face, Ariana cut the article out from the paper and slid it into her folder of clues. She then slipped the folder into the filing cabinet and headed out of the garage. She had to get ready for the engagement party of a very special couple. Tofan *Baba* and Hava Bibi were getting married. Years ago the two had fallen in love as teenagers and had secretly hoped to marry, but their fathers' feud had made that impossible. For fifty years Tofan had remained true to his love for Hava Bibi, and he'd proposed to her the night of Uncle Habib's dinner. And tonight the two families would be united as one.

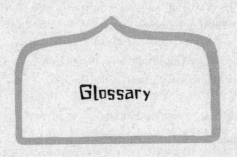

Glossary

alhamdulillah—An Arabic phrase meaning "praise to God."

Allah—Standard Arabic word for God, used by Muslims as well as Arab Christians.

aushak—An Afghan dish made of pasta dumplings filled with leeks, served with a meat sauce and topped with yogurt and dried mint.

baba—Respectful term used for an older man.

bachay—Plural of *"bacha"*; means "children" in Pukhto and Farsi.

badal—Code of blood feuds or revenge in *Pukhtunwali*.

bharata natyam—A classical Indian dance form originating in the south Indian state of Tamil Nadu.

burka—Enveloping outer garment worn by women in some Islamic countries.

chador—A large cloth worn as a combination head covering, veil, and shawl, usually by Muslim women.

chiyogami—A type of *washi* paper featuring woodblock-printed designs depicting Japanese imagery.

dastarkhan—Tablecloth laid out on the ground for family meals, which are traditionally eaten on the floor.

doday—Means "bread" in Pukhto.

Farsi—Persian language spoken in Afghanistan (also called Dari).

ghayrat—Means "sense of honor and pride" in *Pukhtunwali*.

gunzakhil—A type of fried Afghan cookie.

halal—Denoting or relating to food prepared as prescribed by Muslim law, similar to how "kosher" relates to Jewish law.

imandar—The concept that a Pukhtun must always strive for good in thought, word, and deed and must behave respectfully to people, animals, and the environment around them.

*insha'*Allah—An expression meaning "if God wills," used to suggest that something in the future is uncertain.

jaan—Means "love" or "dearest" in Pukhto and Farsi.

Kabul—The capital and largest city of Afghanistan.

kameez—Long tunic or shirt—worn over loose, flowing pants, which are called a *parthuk*.

kami—Means "paper" in Japanese.

kebob—Refers to a variety of meat dishes consisting of grilled or broiled meats on a skewer or stick.

khala—Means "aunt" in Pukhto.

kimchi—A traditional fermented Korean dish made of vegetables with a variety of seasonings.

kosher—sanctioned by Jewish law, especially referring to things that are fit for ritual use.

lablabu—Beets cooked and sold by vendors in Afghanistan and beloved by children for their sweet taste.

leberkäse—Horse meat sausage from Austria.

mantu—A kind of dumpling, usually filled with lamb or beef, that is popular in Afghanistan.

mashahallah—Literally means "whatever God wills." It is often used on occasions when there is surprise at someone's good deeds or achievements.

melmastia—The code of hospitality and protection offered to every guest in *Pukhtunwali*. Guests must set aside their differences if they are feuding.

nang—Display of honor in *Pukhtunwali*.

origami—The Japanese art of folding paper into decorative shapes and figures.

parthuk—Loose-fitting pants worn under a *kameez*.

pastissada—Horse meat stew made in Italy, particularly in Verona.

Pukhto—An Indo-European language spoken primarily by the Pukhtuns.

Pukhtun—The largest ethnic group in Afghanistan, composing 42% of the population. They speak Pukhto.

Pukhtunwali—A concept of living, or philosophy, for the Pukhtun people; it is regarded as an honor code and an unwritten law.

pulao—A dish of cooked rice that contains a variety of meat and vegetables.

sahib—A form of address or a title placed after a man's name or designation, used as a mark of respect.

salaam alaikum—An Arabic spoken greeting used by Muslims as well as Arab Christians and Jews, and means "peace be upon you."

sitar—A large, long-necked Indian lute with movable frets, played with a wire pick.

tabla—A pair of small hand drums used in Indian music.

Taliban—A predominantly Pukhtun movement that governed Afghanistan from 1996 until 2001.

vaastu shastra—The Indian science of architecture and design of temples, homes, and buildings.

walaikum a'salaam—The traditional response to *"salaam alaikum"*; it means "and upon you be peace."

washi—A traditional Japanese paper made from plant fiber. The most widely made type is *kozogami*, made from the mulberry tree.

AUTHOR'S NOTE

In my author's note for *Shooting Kabul*, the companion novel to *Saving Kabul Corner*, I confessed to having resisted writing the book for many years due to two reasons. First, it was a very personal story, loosely based on my husband and his family's escape from Afghanistan after the Soviets invaded in 1979. Second, it dealt with many sensitive issues—the tragic events of 9/11, the war on terror, Islam, and Afghan culture and politics. In the end, with some trepidation, I wrote the story and it went out into the world. Three years later, I've been overwhelmed and humbled by the positive response it has received. What made me most proud were the e-mails and letters I got from kids who found common connections with Fadi, the protagonist, who flees with his family from a Taliban-controlled Afghanistan in 2001, accidentally leaving his younger sister, Mariam, behind. These kids felt that they were being given a glimpse into a part of the world that they knew little about but had often seen in the news, and now they felt that they were able to relate to it on a personal level. I've always felt that if you give young people the opportunity to explore and experience other cultures, they will often realize how much we have in common and, in the process, also appreciate our differences.

Whenever I visited a school or gave a presentation, the question that inevitably came up was: Will you write a story about Mariam? It seemed Mariam's story haunted many readers, and it gave me sleepless nights as well. By the end of 2001, the Taliban had been ousted, al-Qaeda had been dismantled, and Hamid Karzai had been elected president (with US backing), generating renewed hope in a country ravaged by generations of war and instability. So when I decided to write *Saving Kabul Corner*,

I knew Mariam would play a key role, hopefully answering some of the questions that so many kids kept asking about her.

Sadly, as *Saving Kabul Corner* goes to press, Afghanistan remains unstable. President Karzai, who had been elected with great fanfare thirteen years ago, was unable to bring together all the warring factions. Economic conditions improved slightly, but the economy continues to struggle and remains dependent on outside assistance. Corruption remains a problem, opium cultivation has once again escalated, and the Taliban continues to threaten and destabilize the country. While the most recent presidential election that brought Ashraf Ghani to power is a step in the right direction, the drawn-out electoral process and tumultuous tug-of-war with his competitor Abdullah Abdullah are signs that the underlying tensions within the country remain a problem. President Ghani will undoubtedly have his hands full as the United States and NATO withdraw their troops without a long-term security arrangement.

The outlook for the country is unclear. One thing, however, is certain: the feuding sides will have to find a way to address their differences and come together for the good of the country. Even the Taliban, who continue to commit acts of violence, will eventually have to be reintegrated into any future political settlement.

But as I pointed out in the epilogue to my first book, Afghans are a proud, determined, and optimistic people. I hope this optimism and determination, along with a dose of humility, brings peace, security, and prosperity to a country that has been fighting for far too long, *insh'Allah*. No doubt the children of Afghanistan and all future generations are counting on and praying for their success.

—N. H. Senzai, October 2014

FURTHER READING

Books

Ali, Sharifah Enayat. *Afghanistan (Cultures of the World)*. New York: Benchmark Books, 2006.

Banting, Erinn. *Afghanistan the Land (Lands, Peoples, and Cultures)*. New York: Crabtree Publishing Company, 2003.

Bjorklund, Ruth. *Afghanistan (Enchantment of the World. Second Series)*. New York: Scholastic,Children's Press, 2011.

Clements, Andrew. *Extra Credit*. New York: Atheneum, 2009.

Ellis, Deborah. *The Breadwinner Trilogy*. Toronto: Groundwood Books, 2009.

———. *Kids of Kabul: Living Bravely Through a Never-Ending War*. Toronto: Groundwood Books, 2012.

Khan, Rukhsana. *Wanting Mor*. Toronto: Groundwood Books, 2010.

O'Brien, Tony, and Mike Sullivan. *Afghan Dreams: Young Voices of Afghanistan*. New York: Bloomsbury USA Children's Books, 2008.

Owings, Lisa. *Afghanistan (Blastoff! Readers: Exploring Countries)*. Minneapolis: Bellwether Media, 2011.

Reedy, Trent. *Words in the Dust*. New York: Arthur A. Levine Books, 2011.

Weber, Valerie J. *I come from Afghanistan (This Is My Story)*. Pleasantville, NY: Weekly Reader Early Learning Library, 2006.

Whitfield, Susan. *National Geographic Countries of the World; Afghanistan*. Des Moines: National Geographic Children's Books, 2008.

Websites

BBC News Country Profile: Afganistan
bbc.co.uk/news/world-south-asia-12011352

CIA World Factbook
cia.gov/library/publications/the-world-factbook/geos/af.html

National Geographic
kids.nationalgeographic.com/kids/places/find/afghanistan/

Time For Kids
http://www.timeforkids.com/destination/afghanistan

UNICEF
unicef.org/infobycountry/afghanistan.html

World Atlas
worldatlas.com/webimage/countrys/asia/af.htm

About the Book

When her cousin Laila arrives in California from war-torn Afghanistan, twelve-year-old Ariana resents her perfect manners and competence. Ariana's large extended family seems to prefer the gentle newcomer to outspoken Ariana. But Ariana soon has a bigger worry—the grocery store owned by her family is losing business to a new family-owned store nearby. The two families clash and suddenly violence erupts. Figuring out who has caused the violence brings Ariana and Laila together and introduces a new boy into Ariana's life. Fascinating details about Afghan-American food and culture blend with thought-provoking themes about conflict in this fast-paced mystery.

Prereading Questions

Discuss the issue of conflicts, why they occur, and how they can be resolved. Consider conflicts on a small, personal level such as a disagreement with a friend. Consider them also at a broader level such as war.

Before reading the book, look carefully at the Table of Contents and discuss what it foreshadows about the story. Can you predict anything about the genre, plot, characters, or setting? Look also at the glossary at the end of the book and discuss why it might be included.

Discussion Questions

The following questions in this section particularly address the Common Core State Standards for Reading Literature: (RL.4–7.1, 2, 4) (RL.4–6.3) (RL.5–6.5, 6)

1. Ariana envies Laila for a number of reasons, and later learns that Laila envies her. Compare and contrast the two characters. What do they have in common? How are they different? Describe how others in the family such as Hava Bibi, Zayd, and the twins treat each girl, and why.

2. One worry for Ariana is that Mariam and Laila will become best friends. Why does she think that? What do Mariam and Laila share in their lives and in their pasts that Ariana doesn't? How does this problem get resolved in the book?

3. Laila has recently moved to the US from Afghanistan. Throughout the story, she mentions details about her life in Afghanistan, which inform the reader about that country. Describe some of those details including her home life and her education there, and how they contrast with her life in the US.

4. Not long after she meets him, Ariana says some harsh words to Wali. Why is she angry at him? What are the results of her outburst? Describe how and why their relationship changes. By the end of the book, how do they feel about each other?

5. Ariana dislikes most kinds of clothing unless the fabric is very soft. She finds tags scratchy and seams irritating. On the other hand, she enjoys the feel of certain fabrics and papers. Find examples of these reactions in the story. What causes them? Why do you think the author included this as part of Ariana's character?

6. Hava Bibi and Uncle Tofan play important roles in bringing together the two families. Describe how they knew each other, and how they helped bring about peace. How did the book foreshadow what you learn about the two of them in the final paragraph?

7. Ariana and her friends end up solving the mystery of what's happening in their shopping plaza. Lay out the steps they take and the clues they gather. Who were the various suspects? Describe the scene where they find final proof of their theory about who did it. Who were the culprits and why did they work to destroy the businesses?

8. Mariam likes a TV reality show called *Take That*. Describe the show and discuss its similarities to parts of the story. How does the first mention of the show foreshadow certain elements that occur later in the plot? Why did the author use foreshadowing? How does it involve the reader in the mystery?

9. Ariana's extended family is worried about the store but also worried about Laila's father. Describe what he does and what happens to him. As Laila hears about his situation, how does she feel and how does she show those feelings?

10. Ariana is learning about endangered species in school. Describe how she applies that concept to her family's store and the threats against its existence. Explain the parallels between endangered species and the store. What other aspects of her life does Ariana consider endangered? She uses the phrase "survival of the fittest." How does this phrase apply to the situation with the store?

11. Another theme in this novel is conflict. Consider the conflicts between the two families in the past in Afghanistan and in the present about the stores. Ariana also mentions the famous feud between the Hatfields and McCoys. Compare and contrast the conflicts. Are any of them resolved? If so, how? How does the war in Afghanistan affect Ariana's extended family?

12. The novel's point of view is a type of first person narrative called limited omniscient. It conveys Ariana's thoughts but no one else's. Find places in the text that show what Ariana is thinking. Find some of her thoughts that are in italics and others that aren't. What is the difference between the two types? Why does the author sometimes use italics?

13. Many novels, even if they have chapter titles, don't have tables of contents. After you've read the book, look back at the Table of Contents and consider the chapter titles. What do individual chapter titles convey about that chapter? Looking at the order, do the titles give a sense of how the book flows? Why do you think this particular book includes a Table of Contents?

14. *Saving Kabul Corner* ends with an epilogue. What does the epilogue tell you that wasn't in the final chapter before it? Why did the author use a newspaper excerpt instead of just describing what happened or having characters discuss it? What incidents in the book led you to believe there might be a newspaper story about what happened?

15. The author weaves in words and phrases from Arabic, Farsi, and Pukhto. What does this add to the story? How different would the novel be without these words? Find some of the words in the text. Is their meaning clear in the context or is the glossary necessary for understanding them?

16. Besides the words from other languages, this novel has other vocabulary that may be unfamiliar. As you read, write down new words. First, try to understand their meanings from the context. Then look up the words in a dictionary. Here are some possibilities:

roughhousing
inconsequential
temperamental
uptick
bamboozled
premise
deflated
buffeted
retaliate
forcible
Möbius strip
quizzically
cavernous
perpetrated

17. Why do you think the author chose to tell Ariana's story instead of just continuing Mariam and Fadi's from *Shooting Kabul*?

Classroom Activities

Kebobs and Lablabu

Between the grocery store and family meals, this story mentions many different foods such as kebobs and lablabu (sugared beets). As a class, make a list of foods that are mentioned, using the narrative and glossary. Each student can choose a type of food to learn more about. They can present their findings to the class orally or as a poster with information, photographs found online, and recipes. If possible, the class could cook some of the food together or students could bring food in that they cooked or bought. Use the topic as a way to discuss foods from different cultures, emphasizing similarities as well as differences.

Crossroads of the Ancient World

Students may think of Afghanistan mainly as a war-torn country. But, as *Saving Kabul Corner* makes clear, it is also a region, sometimes called the Crossroads of the Ancient World, with a rich history and cultural heritage. To get an overview of that heritage, students should visit the National Geographic for Kids website listed below, which has a slide show, video, map, and a printable card with information. Students should choose different topics about ancient or modern Afghanistan for a research project to do alone or in pairs, using both print and digital resources to find information. The author provides a bibliography and websites at the back of the book. The final product could be both a paper and a short presentation to the class in which students share their findings.

National Geographic for Kids:
http://kids.nationalgeographic.com/kids/places/find/afghanistan

Guide written by Kathleen Odean, a former school librarian and Chair of the 2002 Newbery Award Committee. She gives professional development workshops on books for young people and is the author of Great Books for Girls *and* Great Books about Things Kids Love.

This guide, written to align with the Common Core State Standards (www.corestandards'org) has been provided by Simon & Schuster for classroom, library, and reading group use. It may be reproduced in its entirety or excerpted for these purposes.